W0007613

William Wall

William Wall grew up in the coastal village of Whitegate in County Cork and took a degree in Philosophy and English at University College Cork. His first novel *Alice Falling* was published by Sceptre to critical acclaim in 1999. He has won the American Ireland Prize for short stories.

Besides his fiction he has won three major awards for poetry including the Patrick Kavanagh Award. His collection *Mathematics & Other Poems* appeared in 1997.

Minding Children

WILLIAM WALL

SCEPTRE

First published in Great Britain in 2001 by Hodder and Stoughton
A division of Hodder Headline

A Sceptre Paperback

10 9 8 7 6 5 4 3 2 1

A CIP catalogue record for this title
is available from the British Library.

ISBN 0 340 75190 8

Typeset by Hewer Text Ltd, Edinburgh
Printed and bound in Great Britain by
Mackays of Chatham plc, Chatham, Kent

Hodder and Stoughton
A division of Hodder Headline
338 Euston Road
London NW1 3BH

for David Marcus

ONE

Josephine Strane carried her bags like ungainly carcasses. The wind caught them and turned them, scraping her legs and catching in things she passed. She leaned slightly forwards to keep the hood of her duffle coat over her face but the rain still beat coldly on her nose and lips. When she licked her tongue over them she could taste the cold and the salt. Robin's socks were full of salt that time he walked in the water. She rinsed them in the sink and saw the scum coming out, the scum of the sea. Billie Fraser didn't like it, she knew, not her son Robin walking in the water with his shoes on. Who killed cock Robin? That was a song. And what was the answer? A sparrow.

The wind came at her through the gullies of the buildings, blowing up from the sea, with sea-spray and leaves and plastic bags on it. The naked cherry trees rustled their papery fingers.

Lights were on in every house. The streets were lit in flickering amber, the poles shivering and swinging. Creaking rain arrived in sudden, horizontal, piercing gusts. Hurricane Mona, born late in the year in the warm waters of the tropics, was gradually coming to rest on the south coast of Ireland, having swung through the eastern seaboard of the United States and then veered crazily across the Atlantic. Now it was spending the last of its strength in shaking windows and bringing down power cables. She remembered seeing its image on a television screen in Bolster's Electrical Appliances window, a white swirl like one of Robert Fraser's secret numbers, a twist of violence in a blackness that signified the ocean.

And they call the wind Maria, she thought. That was a song. High-pitched women's voices, the screaming wind, an urgent relentless rhythm. Women's names for storms. Whipping the sea into a fury, throwing up old bones and sticks and dead fish, everything disordered. The delicate lines of the beach where she saw the boy swimming, the sand blown by the wind into wrinkles; a storm would tear it all away. Sand blows into the eyes but never let water into them. Death comes in there. The head floats.

She thought of the dogfish-skin of the dead child and the jelly-skin of the man who died pissing over the side of the boat. That was years ago. And the girl that liked touching their things. She was glad that was all behind her. She had vowed that she would never go for boys again. She shuddered and the shudder became a shivering.

2

Cold.

Have to get in out of the cold. Last night there was the thing to do with that man and then the last night in the bandstand. A warm one for a change, the calm before the storm they said. And Susan was lying on her bed all this time, hands arranged at her side, eyes clicked closed. Hear no evil, see no evil, speak no evil. That was one of Auntie Mary's.

She came to a street that was on a gently sloping hill. The houses were suddenly better kept, separated from the street by a small garden, a wall of pointed stone topped by a low ornamental rail with cast-iron spikes that sheltered a tiny green lichen in their grooves. Their lawns were smooth and bordered by select shrubs and overblown perennials – the last blackening dahlias, miniature pampas looking like unwashed hair. The fluff came away in your hand and stuck to clothes.

Halfway along the street she stopped to exchange bags and hands, the most awkward, heaviest-looking bag going from right to left. She looked up and saw, in the bay window of a red-brick house, a golden room in which moved a young woman and a man and a boy of a year or two. The room was lit by four lamps on tables and a bright fire. A television flickered blue in the background, some old film on it, a woman looking down from high tiled roofs on a Spanish courtyard. Josephine struggled to identify the scene but the screen was too far away.

The man moved in front of it and folded to his knees and the child rushed at him. When the child hit him the father fell backwards, tumbling, a clown all hands and legs. The woman was laughing. The golden light warmed the shrubs that pressed close to the window and gradually lost its potency as it stretched across the lawn towards the rails. Josephine Strane stared at the repetitious game, her eyes watchful, darting, her face, creased by the wind, slowly relaxing, a softness smoothing it like sand levelled by an encroaching tide. She watched the man's open-armed anticipation, the child's intense concentration, the woman's erupting laughter. When the woman finally broke the cycle and drew the curtains Josephine made a noise between a grunt and a growl, and shook her head twice rapidly like a bird. Then she moved on, trudging up the street.

Everything around her seemed to resonate now in the increasing fury of the storm. The sound of the wind was the sound of houses struggling to breathe, the sound of trees leaning and straightening, the sound of cars splashing past, the whistling wires, gates creaking or banging, rain driving on the ground, on her hood, on her back. She was at sea in sound, drowning in watery air. She felt choked, a swimmer struggling towards a distant surface. She even looked upwards for the diaphanous skin, hoping for a breaking light above her, but there was only the rain-filled lamplight and beyond that the emptiness of the invisible sky.

Near the top of the street – from where if she stood on tiptoe she would be able to make out the distant lighthouse, the trawlers groaning at their warps – she turned into a gateway, nudging it open with her hip, swung her bags through and nudged it closed again. She stood at the front door and wondered for a moment which bag to put down. She settled for the left one, leaning it carefully against the frame of the door. She pressed the doorbell and waited. As she waited she shuffled from foot to foot.

After a time a light went on in the hall inside. The door opened and a woman looked out, and a gust of air came out too, laden with the smell of take-away food, something Chinese. In the back-light of the hall she looked yellow, the colour of turf ash. Her hair was lank and greasy. Her eyes were puffy. She glared for a moment. Then made a sound like that of an animal disturbed in its sleep.

'I came to say I'm sorry,' Josephine Strane said. She remembered the day she had first seen her: tall and willowy, black hair tied back, very American in her slacks and sweater.

Sorry for your trouble, she should have said.

Sorry to hear the news.

That was the way to say it. The mourners at the funeral years ago, they came along the front bench of the church and shook hands with her mother, with her. Sorry for your trouble. Sorry for your trouble. It was to make things better, because grief belonged to everyone. Her mother was slumped a little in the seat, otherwise you couldn't tell. And all these days she had wanted the same ritual, ever since the day she had seen Robin go up to the Protestant graveyard. She didn't think Protestants would say it like that, Mr Minister and his wife, a cold fish. She had wanted to say the words ever since she saw the white coffin, grief a demon clamouring within.

Poor Robin, God rest him. Sorry for your trouble.

'You can't come in.' It was a bald statement, cold water thrown in the face of sympathy. Josephine picked up the second plastic bag as though to get ready for a quick escape. 'Please. Can I talk to Mr Fraser?'

The woman shook her head twice. She seemed to be paralysed below the neck.

Josephine Strane stepped closer, almost into the door.

'Robert?' she said. 'Just for a minute?' Robert Fraser would understand. She was bringing them their safety, the prize of order and routine. She would be their saviour now, taking the pith of their lives and giving it a shell, a carapace that would keep the world out. Now more than ever they needed her.

Again the woman shook her head, quizzically now.

'Yes?' Josephine Strane said. 'Please.'

The woman stepped back a little. It was a surrender and Josephine Strane stepped into the hall. 'I brought food. Three French sticks. A chicken. A bottle of wine for you. Some cheese.' She would come round in time. She would not hold out against her. 'I'm sorry for your trouble, Mrs Fraser,' Josephine said.

'I can't bear it,' the woman said. 'Too much. Too many things to remember.'

'I have no place to go,' Josephine Strane said. 'I slept in the bandstand this week past. But I can't sleep in the rain. I have no money left.'

'That's got nothing to do with us.'

'It wasn't my fault. It was an accident. I warned you he was always running away.'

The woman's face wrinkled suddenly and her eyes closed almost completely. She bit her lips.

'Can't you leave us alone –' she choked on the word, her right hand going symbolically to her throat. She drew breath again. '– to our grief.'

'I'm sorry too but I know I must stay calm.'

'Dear God.'

A door closed somewhere in the house and at the same time the assault of the wind became violent. Something noisy broke away outside and clattered along the road. A garden gate began to bang. At the same time the air screamed in every opening – under the loose window-sashes, under the door, through key-holes, down chimneys. They were silent for a moment as though hearing the wind for the first time.

'Did you know my Uncle Jimmy was lost at sea?' Josephine said. She was beginning to feel happy. Everything would be all right, she felt. Things would be better.

Unexpectedly the woman said, 'My Robin.' She gulped and gazed at Josephine.

Josephine Strane nodded her head. She smiled comfortingly.

'Least said soonest mended, as my Auntie Mary used to say. I'll cook the chicken. The way I did it one night. In the stone casserole with onions and herbs. I'll make garlic bread.' She looked around her at the disarray of the house, the smell of old food and damp clothes, the sense of abandonment. It's true what they say, she thought, when a child is gone from a house the heart goes out of it. She would change that, if only for a time. She would bring them cleanliness and routine. She would help them to piece their lives together. Then she would move on. That was the way she was. She had done the same for Dr Casey. She would do it for anyone. It was her nature.

The woman took her hand away from her throat and made a fist of it. It was a small, unconvincing fist. She looked at it herself and opened it slowly. She shook her head and turned away, climbing the stairs slowly and painfully. She did not turn again.

Josephine Strane closed the door behind her and went down the hall to the kitchen. She saw the light on in the front room where Robert Fraser had his study. She knew he would be sitting at his desk. She did not think he would be working. *The Undecidable*, she thought, Martin Davis, Raven Press. *Number the Language of Science*, Tobias Danzig. All the magic names. His books. He would be staring at the window watching the loom of the lighthouse, the strip of sea and rain plucked out of nothing by its rotation.

The blank distance.

She put her bags down on the draining board and looked around her at the tiny kitchen. The pine table had bread-crumbs and some indefinable stain like milked coffee or chocolate that had got into the grain. There were pots and dirty dishes in the sink and the cooker was black where something had boiled over on the ceramic plates. She pursed her lips. Robin's scrawled drawings were still Sellotaped to the door of the fridge – a big face with an open mouth, some kind of black insect that he claimed was a bee, a dog with three and a half legs, a fish with something trailing out of it. She took off her duffle coat and hung it on a hook behind the door. She looked at the drawings one by one, laughing at the dog. She rolled her sleeves up and in ten minutes she had washed and cleaned the pots and swept the table clean. She took the food out of its bags and spread it on the pine table. She took the stone casserole from a kitchen press and filled it with cold water. She peeled two onions and studded them with cloves. She sliced the garlic and crushed it with the flat of the knife. She pushed the garlic into butter and whipped them into a paste with a fork.

She stripped the wrapping from the chicken and dropped it on to the chopping board. The legs fell open and Josephine laughed and said, 'Like a baby's bottom.' She patted it lovingly. Then she shoved the onions inside, two translucent mines vanishing in a tunnel. She coated the skin with the butter. She put the chicken in the stone casserole and opened the bottle of wine. She opened a tin of tomatoes and poured it over the chicken, singing as she worked. 'But it was in the early spring, when flowers bloom and robins sing, she went away.' She poured wine over the chicken. 'And Honey I miss you, and I'm feeling blue.' She covered it and put it in the oven. When she turned to finish the garlic bread Robert Fraser was standing in the kitchen door staring at her.

'Hi Robert,' she said. 'Did you get much work done?'

'Who let you in?'

'Were you working on your book?'

'Do you think I have work on my mind at this time!'

'Life must go on.' She winked. 'Honey I miss you and I'm feeling blue. Bobby Goldsborough.'

'You better go.'

'I'm cooking your dinner. Your favourite. Remember? The chicken casserole. And Robin's.'

She lifted the wine bottle and shook it slightly, an arch smile. It was an invitation. 'I have no place to go,' she said. 'I can't sleep in the bandstand tonight.'

'You can't stay in this house.' He made an ineffectual gesture with his left hand, as though indicating the impossibility of these walls containing her, these rooms, her presence an impossibility.

'Will I pour you a glass?'

He seemed to consider it for a ludicrous instant, his eyes studying it like an equation. 'Look, you can't stay. Not after all this. I remember you said you had a family at the interview. Go and live with them.'

She shook her head sadly. 'I lied,' she said. 'I wanted the job badly. There's not many jobs for child-minders and it's my vocation. Sure, all my family are dead anyway. I only ever had an aunt. I never saw my mother, let alone my father.'

'You lied?' he asked, shaking his head as though to clear it, his eyes sharply predatory, hunting for insight.

'I had to.'

'You went to see your mother once? We gave you two days off.'

Josephine Strane watched him silently.

'Your sister?'

'Give up,' she said. She smiled happily as though he were playing twenty questions.

'What about Robin?' he asked. It was almost a whisper. His eyes narrowed as though he were trying to read hers, but her round face and brown eyes gave no sign, no morsed blink signalled unease. 'Poor Robin, God rest him,' she said.

He too turned and walked away. 'Don't worry,' she called after him. 'I'm looking around for something else.' She heard the study door close. She laughed and a new song came to her. She began to sing in a high-pitched girlish lilt, her voice carrying through the door and the hall and up the stairs – 'Take a chance on me, take a chance on me.' As she sang she did a small tight dance routine that involved stepping backwards and forwards rhythmically and moving her hands in constricted circles in unison. She flicked her head a little at each beat, but her face remained expressionless and unchanging, self-absorbed. She sang for a few moments in the solemn dance, then she stopped abruptly. She took up one of the breads and paused to listen to the rain beating against the kitchen window. 'It's so snug,' she said aloud. 'In here out of the rain.'

She switched on the small stereo that stood in the cover of the overhanging presses and heard the metallic jingle of the local radio station timing up to the news. 'And in the day's top story . . .' The breathless voice of the newsreader reeled off snippets about the death of Chairman Mao, the by-election in England and a story about a soccer player. 'And now for the local stories. A mentally handicapped man has been found in a distressed state on the waterfront. It is understood the man, who has been taken into Health Board custody, was found locked into the gents' toilet near the bandstand at about nine o'clock this morning. Gardaí say they are . . .' She flicked the switch again and the radio went dead. 'Looking into the matter,' Josephine said. She smiled.

TWO

There was an aunt – Auntie Mary, spinster, fifty years of age, hair of silver grey, a tendency to talk to herself. Two rooms on the ground floor, three on the first, including the toilet. Josephine called each Saturday morning with a bag of messages from the shop. It was a ritual list, a litany of the unblessed virgin: bread, butter, tea, sugar, Buckfast Tonic Wine, a quarter of boiled sweets, a piece of meat for the dinner, a bone for the dog, *Woman's Weekly* and the *Far East*. One Saturday Josephine opened the front door to silence. She listened, head cocked to one side at the front door, right hand dangling a net bag, a yellow-faced doll tucked under her left. Auntie Mary did not shuffle in her loose slippers. Josephine looked into the parlour and the kitchen and saw they were empty. She put her messages on the kitchen table and the Buckfast Tonic Wine tipped over on its side and would have rolled off except that she leaned her belly against the table's edge and stopped it. It was late summer and the flies buzzed at the thickened milkstains, the crumbs. A bare white bone on a willow-pattern plate attracted three bluebottles. Somewhere outside in the heat of the morning the dog would be sleeping.

'Auntie Mary,' she called. 'It's me. Josephine. I've brought the messages.' Auntie Mary did not reply.

The staircase creaked and groaned. Under the first plank of the fifth step, Josephine knew, her aunt kept her money and the title deeds to the house. 'I'm going to show you where the deeds are,' she used to say, 'in case anything happens to me. You'll know. You're the only one.' In the dusty darkness of the step was a tin box and a roll of pound notes. 'You can keep the money,' her aunt said. 'You'll be rich. You needn't tell anyone about it. I know you're well able to lie. But the deeds must go to my brother in America.'

'But Auntie,' she would say in the early days, 'Uncle Jimmy died in the war.'

'A lie is a big black X on your soul,' Auntie Mary would say. 'Tell the truth and shame the devil.'

'But my Mam always says . . .'

'Put your hand on your heart,' Auntie Mary would say, 'and swear by Almighty God that you will never tell a lie again.' Sometimes she would take a battered prayerbook full of tiny photographs of dead people and short prayers. 'Put your hand on the missal and say after me, I swear by Almighty God and by the Blessed Virgin Mary and by all the Saints that I will give up my wicked habit of slander and lies.'

After the swearing came the test. 'Did you mean it?' she would say. 'If you did you will never tell a lie again. Otherwise you will go straight to hell if you die. You could drop dead this minute. Or a car could roll over you.' She would pause for a time. 'Did you go to the toilet yet?' she might ask. If Josephine said yes her aunt might say, 'Tell me what it was.' If she said no her aunt might keep her in the house for hours. It was a truth-test, she said. The more embarrassing it was, the better the test.

'Show me how you wash yourself,' and Josephine would have to mime the process of washing herself. 'Cleanliness is next to godliness,' her aunt would say. She would watch the process intently, as though observing an actual event. 'Keep yourself clean all over child.'

'Your mother was never the cleanest,' she would say. 'She always had bad habits.'

Sometimes she would examine Josephine's clothes. She would check the collar of her blouse and if there was a film of oil on it she would make Josephine take it off. She would scrub the collar in a basin of water and hang it in front of the fire to dry. Sometimes Josephine would be made to sit shivering in the kitchen until the washing was finished and then put on her wet blouse as a punishment for wearing something dirty. The collar hung like coarse wet rope around her neck. She took to bringing a spare pair of panties in case her aunt found fault with them. More than once she had been sent home to change them.

Once she said, 'Do you know the right way to sleep child?' Josephine Strane said, 'No Auntie.'

'Like this,' her aunt said. She sat back in her chair and folded her hands in an X across her chest, high up at her breastbone. 'This is the right way. Keep the hands outside the blankets. You'll only scratch and tear yourself if you have the hands inside.'

'You wouldn't scratch in your sleep,' Josephine said.

'You would,' her aunt said. 'It's a human instinct. It leads to sin.' She had to practise sleeping with her hands crossed. Her aunt hovered behind her adjusting the position of her hands and straightening her legs until she was satisfied. 'That's the right way,' she said. She knew, she said, that Josephine had no way of knowing these things because her mother was an ignorant featherbrain. Then she would ask Josephine whether her mother was teaching her the catechism or preparing her for confirmation, or saying the rosary with her. Josephine usually lied.

'We say it every night,' she would say, but her aunt would fly into a temper, her face reddening, a livid glow displacing the pale cracks and fissures and the small black dots of hopeless pores. 'Liar!' she would shout. 'Dirty filthy liar!' And then the business of swearing would begin all over again.

Her aunt said that the air was full of what she called 'spoors' of disease. She would point to the blue-grey mould that grew on a bulge of plaster in the corner of the kitchen. 'No matter what I scrub it with it comes back,' she said. 'Parazone even. You can't kill that stuff.' Auntie Mary said the house was mortared with sea-sand, which everyone knows makes dampness. Sometimes you could see the crystals gleaming with moisture, a salt crust extruded, water plucked mysteriously from the air. Sometimes the kitchen smelled like the wet sand at the high-tide mark. The spoors blew into the air and circulated around your body, she said. They got in everywhere. Josephine imagined tiny fungal stains on her insides, in her private places, in the lining of her nose and her ears. Sometimes, at night, she would put her hands over them to block the ingress. She would wake from her sleep and find her hands on her ears.

'Wait until Uncle Jimmy comes home,' Auntie Mary would say at other times. 'He'll straighten you out. He won't put up with no nonsense.' Sometimes she would take a snap from her missal and show it to Josephine. It showed two girls and a boy linking arms, standing awkwardly for the camera, crooked grins and mischievous eyes. One was her mother, thin then, with bulging cheekbones and full bee-stung lips. She wore something smart, something very like what Jeant Leigh or Grace Kelly might wear in an old black and white picture on television. The other was Auntie Mary, head a tangle of wiry hair, huge-chested, wearing something close to a hessian bag for a dress.

The boy was taller than both of them, already jaunty although he did not join the Navy for another two years, Auntie Mary said. There was something cold about him, something that disturbed Josephine every time she saw the snap. 'Oh he was the boyo for straightening out,' Auntie Mary would say. 'The things he did to me.'

But Uncle Jimmy was lost at sea, so he could not have been so good at straightening things out. Josephine thought of him wandering in his boat in the kind of clammy fog that drifted in from the sea on summer days, or swimming out there, miles out in the ocean, his clothes icy and heavy and clinging to his body, unable to decide where the land was, unable to return home to straighten her out.

At the top of the stairs was a picture of the Sacred Heart, the lurid red glow of the heart and the guttering glow of the nightlight. Christ's hands were pressed to his chest to show the red slits in the back that were his wounds. Auntie Mary said that she would bleed herself when the time came every month and this was a reminder of Christ's wounds. Josephine thought that God's eyes were soft and worried-looking. When they followed her movements she imagined that He was hoping that she would do the right thing.

Josephine found her aunt in bed. The room was full of soft light and the waving shadows of an elder tree that grew outside the window. A loud fly buzzed against blinds and swung crazily around the room when Josephine moved in. 'Auntie,' she said. The fly landed on her aunt's mouth and disappeared inside for a moment. It emerged a second later and moved across her upper lip and on to her cheek in tiny darting movements. The fly was a rich metallic blue. Its body gleamed like heated steel.

'You're dead,' Josephine said. Her skin prickled all over, a warm rush of excitement. She watched the fly's alacrity, his tiny bustle, saw him linger in the hairs of her aunt's upper lip where a faint powdery down of milk still showed. The empty glass was on the bedside table.

She walked around the room and touched things, moved the hairbrush and rearranged the small armchair so that light from the window fell upon it at a better angle. She sat down and then stood up again, feeling suddenly as if she owned everything she could see, the sole possessor, the mistress. This house was hers, the things in it, the body of her aunt, the fly.

'I'd better wash my hands,' she told her aunt. She placed the doll beside her aunt's face and the doll's eyes clicked shut. 'You mind Auntie, Susan,' she said. She picked up a *Woman's Own* from the bedside table. She opened the letters page.

Josephine liked the cracked adamantine cold of the bathroom: the Shires bowl, the square hospital-sized sink, the cold brass taps visibly attached to greening copper pipes. The bathroom was full of small sounds. The hot tap always ran, a brown streak like melted chocolate marking its course over the varicose cracks. From somewhere overhead came the drizzle of a faulty stopcock, the cistern constantly filling and dribbling water out through the overflow on to the concrete floor of the backyard. The base of the bath was discoloured by years of sheets soaked in bleach. The warmest thing in the room was the whitened oak toilet seat. She sat down, balancing against its tendency to slip sideways and drop her on the floor.

'My husband is very loving,' she read, 'but we haven't been intimate for four years. We had a stillbirth at that time. I love him very much but I can't bear having him touch me. Recently he has started to go out most nights of the week. He says he likes to go for a drink with his mates. Am I driving him away? Please help me. Doris, Middlesex.' On the opposite page there was a beautiful photograph in sepia of a young man and woman on their wedding day. The frame of the photograph was ornate, gilt. The man was wearing a smart double-breasted jacket of the kind that the gangsters wore in 1930s films. The girl was holding a bunch of flowers made black by the darkness of the photograph. 'Who will care for her when I'm gone?' the advertisement asked. The answer was the Sun Life Assurance Company.

She put the magazine down on the edge of the bath and washed her hands. Her aunt always had two soaps. One was a red block of Lifebuoy. She said it was a disinfectant. The other was a thin oblong of greenish-veined Palmolive. The Palmolive reminded Josephine of her aunt's hands. She used the Lifebuoy, scrubbing her palms with it, scouring between her fingers. She opened the cold tap and watched the water run off, the colour of diluted blood.

She turned the tap off, feeling it grate in the last stages, metal on metal. She could not choke off the water entirely. A thin jet still came at an angle. She tried again with both hands and this time she reduced it to a fat drip.

She went to the stairs and saw that the nightlight was guttering. She took it out of its holder and stood it on the top step. She opened the fifth step and stood the board to one side. She took out the tin box and opened it up. There was the thin roll of pound notes, ten perhaps or fifteen, bound with a piece of brittle rubber that broke with a dull snap when she disturbed it. The piece of paper was a yellowed letter. Josephine could not read the writing on it. She brought the letter to the top step and held it over the nightlight. She watched the flame blacken the edge and then catch. She made a small yelping sound and dropped the burning taper. The letter curled up, a thin orange flame briefly sustained by its own substance. Then it was a fragile curve that broke into air-light fragments under her fingers.

She lifted her dress and folded back the rim of her panties and placed the one pound notes against her belly, against the thin fuzz of her pubic hair. She had begun to hum and the humming eventually turned into a song. 'He held a knife up to my breast and into my arms he pressed, I cried my love don't you murder me, I'm not prepared for eternity.' She stood up and went to look at her aunt again. She had not moved. Susan still slept peacefully. The fly was gone. She noticed that her aunt's hands were inside the sheets. She did not have the X on her breastbone.

THREE

Josephine's mother walked behind the hearse as it climbed the hill to the old graveyard. There was no need for a car, she said, never mind the expense. But there were others who drove, the purring engines following on their heels, unnerving. Josephine's mother turned every once in a while and glared at them. One or two had offered her a lift and she had refused. 'I'm not getting into any cars,' she said. 'Not in daylight anyway. Bad enough the rest of the time.' Mary was a rotten old bitch, her mother said, who had her Communion money still and should have left something to her family. She said that Josephine should have kept a closer eye on the old bitch to see where she kept it.

'And I having to bury her,' she said. 'As if I could afford it.' Her mother had been in Clancy's pub since early morning and her breath reeked of whiskey. 'Where had she the money? In some bank account. But where had she the bank book, the dirty whore.' She stumbled frequently and Josephine had to support her by the arm. The road was interminable, pocked with holes that her mother didn't see, yellowed water in the bottom splashing up every time a foot went in. Cattle had crossed the road between two gates just below the graveyard and there was the reek of dung and the green stains to be negotiated, her mother resistant to any change of direction, then careering unsteadily for a time.

'You were up there all the time,' her mother said. 'Did she ever say a word to you?' Josephine shook her head. 'About the money? Did she every say where she had it hid?'

Josephine said that Auntie Mary never talked about money.

'She was a tight bitch!' Her mother slapped her hands together in exasperation. 'By Jesus she was tight all right.'

Josephine said that Auntie Mary was very holy and spent most of her time saying the rosary and that when she went up she had to say the rosary too and pray for the souls of all the people they knew. Her mother said that Mary was a dried up old bitch that deserved to dance on the flags of hell. 'Rosary my arse,' she said. Josephine looked back but the faces behind the windscreens were impassive, and of course they couldn't hear through the glass and the sound of the engine. Let the dead bury the dead, she thought. That was one of Auntie Mary's, but what did it mean?

The hearse stopped at the grassy verge outside the main gate and the mourners spread out among the headstones in a ragged circle around the open grave. Josephine saw that there were pieces of rotten timber thrown on a mound of ochre earth. That was the colour of her grandmother who died before she was born, the colour of death. And her mother's skin had the ochre in it too, partly because she was old and partly because she never went outdoors in daylight if she could help it. Susan's skin was a little yellowed. Her mother's voice calling her from sleep. 'Look what the nice man brought you.' The nice man looked down at her and out of the gloom of his hands came an apple-cheeked smile and a halo of organdie and Josephine saw that it was a doll with eyes that winked on the movement of a balance inside her head. She could hear the balance clink when the doll lay down. That was the first time she saw Susan. And Auntie Mary's eyes were closed, not because of a balance, but because she was dead. Susan would never die.

The priest chanted the prayers, his voice running up and down the scale, answered by the deep-throated murmur of the mourners. As he prayed he gazed into the middle distance and his fingers held the page of his breviary down.

In a short time the ceremony was over and four men stepped forwards, two undertakers dressed in sombre black suits, two gravediggers in overalls and heavy boots. They slid ropes under the coffin and took the weight. They hoisted it up and two men straddled the open grave then transferred to the other side. They lowered the ropes hand over hand. When the top of the box was almost level with the surface one rope slipped and the coffin tipped forwards and downwards. There was a hollow thud. The leg end of the coffin was jammed against the side of the grave. Auntie Mary was going in feet first, Josephine thought.

'Jaysus she's wedged,' one of the men said. Someone in the crowd tittered. The priest's mouth hung open.

'I'll have to get down and get the rope back,' another said. He was the one who had let the rope slip. 'We'll have to pull her up all over again.' He knelt down on the edge of the grave and put his left leg down on the coffin. He looked up at the undertakers and winked. 'Now we'll find out how good is the box,' he said. 'Best oak, hah?'

He stood down on the box and tested it with his weight. 'So far, so good.' He bent down and came up with the rope. 'That's it now,' he said. 'I have it under her again.' He levered himself out of the grave and took up the slack on the rope. He and his opposite number pulled but the coffin did not come up. 'Pull together,' he said. 'All of us.'

The coffin came out of the grave at a crazy angle. Once it was at the surface again they levelled the ropes and lowered it down. It went in smoothly and quietly. The men pulled the ropes clear and dusted their hands together in satisfaction.

'I'm sorry for your trouble, Betty,' the man who had stood on the coffin said. The others came up and shook hands and said similar things. They shook Josephine's hand too.

'Poor old Mary,' one of them said. 'She never did anyone any harm.' Another said that she kept herself to herself but that she was a good neighbour. 'She was the kind of wan that you could expect to last longer than any of us,' an elderly man said. 'I remember when she was a slip of a thing. She was contrary even then.'

Josephine wandered off among the headstones once the talking started, trying to lose herself, hiding and seeking. Out of sight out of mind, as Auntie Mary used to say. She noticed that many of the stones had her name on them. Strane. Ann Strane dearly beloved wife of Michael Strane departed this life 5 October 1876 Requiescat in Pace. James Patrick Strane lost at sea 1943. Eleanor Strane b. 1911 d. 1914 RIP. James Patrick Strane was Uncle Jimmy that her aunt believed was alive and well and living in America, the person to whom the deeds of the house were to go. Her mother never talked about the family. Josephine thought of the brief flaring of the yellowed letter, a lifetime of ownership reduced to a tissue of charcoal.

'Plenty of Stranes up here,' someone said. She turned and saw a dapper man with oiled black hair and a tweed jacket. She had seen him before. Once, when she woke up on a Monday morning he was there for his breakfast, her mother hurrying her to get out to school. There were three greasy rashers and a slice of fried bread on his plate and the kitchen was full of the smell of dripping and steam. He looked at her that morning and did not smile. She remembered things like that. His big hand poised above the cup, a fork in the other. His mouth was moving and she knew that if he opened it she would see the reddish mince of rasher flesh and fat in a lump on his tongue.

'You're looking for someone, are you?'

'I'm looking for my father.' Not even a shadowy shape in the back of her memory. Her mother never talked. Who was my father? Never you mind girl.

The man laughed. 'You won't find him.'

'This is where all the Stranes are buried.'

'What difference does that make? Do you want a fag?' He took out a packet of Players and lit one. 'His name wasn't Strane anyway.'

'My mother is.'

'That's her name all right.'

'Who was he?'

The man laughed. 'Take your pick.' He sucked hard at the cigarette and uttered a pale blue cloud. 'Come over here.' He led her towards the limestone wall, the gable end of a church that once dominated the graveyard. She wondered if her father was lurking behind it, just out of sight of the funeral. But there was no one waiting for them. She felt a tiny disappointment.

When the wall was between them and the mourners he stopped and handed her the cigarette. 'Have a pull,' he said.

Josephine took the cigarette and put it to her lips. She sucked on it and blew the smoke out again. The man laughed. 'You have to suck it down to here,' he said, tapping his chest. 'Look.'

He took it back and sucked on it so that the tip glowed bright red and a pellet of grey ash lengthened and fell away. He held his breath a moment, an ecstatic look in his eyes, then exhaled noisily. Almost no smoke came out. 'I know your mother,' he said. 'Herself and myself were great once.' He sucked on the cigarette again and rocked backwards on his heels. The front of his jacket was shiny as if there were a fine film of oil or polish on it, and the cuffs were frayed and the stitching showed through in places. A whiter piece of stone over his head had 1587 carved on it in florid letters and words in a different language. What did they mean?

'Give us a kiss,' he said. He put his hand on her forearm. The hand had the cigarette poised in the fork between its fingers. The fingers were mustard yellow. She stared at him. 'I'll give you the packet of fags and a lighter,' he said. He put his other hand in his trouser pocket and took out a shiny metal lighter. He flicked the top of the lighter and a flame appeared. He waved it slowly in front of her eyes then let the top fall back into place to extinguish the flame. She nodded. She pursed her lips and inclined her head.

'Not one of them,' he said. 'A real one.' He thought for a moment. 'Like the ones in the pictures. With the mouth open.'

Josephine heard her mother's voice. 'I'm wanted,' she said. 'My mother's calling me.'

He sighed. 'Fair enough,' he said. 'Some other time.'

'See you,' she said. He flicked the lighter at another

cigarette and then put it in his pocket. 'I'll keep it for you,' he said.

The crowd was almost gone. One or two cars were pulling off the verge, people calling to each other, doors slamming. The gravediggers were already scraping the earth sideways on to the coffin, the yellow subsoil first, saving the darker fertile stuff till the last, a thin mound of it to one side full of the pale finger-flesh rhizomes of nettles. Josephine's mother was talking to the priest. When Josephine came up he smiled and patted her head. 'Confirmation this year?' he asked. Josephine said yes. 'A strong and perfect Christian,' the priest said. 'Tell me this now. What name will you take? For confirmation?'

Josephine said that she would take Susan.

The priest looked astonished. 'Where did you get that one?'

'That's a stupid name,' her mother said. 'It has to be a Saint's name or a Bible name.'

'What about Patricia?' the priest said. 'Would you like Patricia? That was the name my mother took, God rest her.'

Josephine said she didn't mind.

'Or Mary after your aunt? And of course our Blessed Mother?'

'I don't mind.'

'Go for Mary. That's what I'd do.'

They turned and walked towards the gate. The priest had coloured streamers on his arm and a large book caught in the crook of his wrist. He was slightly lame, as though one shoe was too tight. 'Anyhow she's getting big,' he said. 'You know what I mean. I don't mind now but I don't think secondary will do her any good. Mrs Casey was only asking me the other day. A young willing girl, says she. Someone to do the bit of housework and mind the child. Mrs Casey would be a good influence on her and she'd be learning a trade so to speak. That wouldn't do her any harm. She's not too young for that kind of thing. I'll talk to the Master and we'll see about keeping her on the roll until she's of age.'

'All right Father.'

'The baby is one. Dr Casey is a busy man and so is herself. Bed and board. She said light housekeeping duties and minding the baby. I believe the baby is only gorgeous. Father White christened her. That was the time I was away, there last year or so. She'll be still on the books until fourteen of course. I'll look after that. Mr Kenneally will do that for me.'

'All right Father.'

'She'll be marked absent if anyone turns up to ask. The inspector. A bit of a white lie. A small white lie.'

'No one minds that.'

'Not at all. A venial sin. Anyhow it's for her own good. It happens all the time. What's the point of keeping someone like your Josephine in school until she's fourteen. And secondary would be no use at all at all.'

The priest got into his car. 'I'm going the other way,' he said. 'So I can't give you a lift.'

'Sure it's only a short walk Father.'

'I'll tell Mrs Casey so.'

'Do Father.'

'And I'll look after the other thing.'

'Right Father.'

'It won't stop the confirmation anyhow.'

He rolled up the window and started the car. As he pulled out he tipped the horn. The braying sound echoed back from the gravestones. Josephine thought it was like Judgement Day when Gabriel would blow his trumpet and the dead would come back. She wondered what Auntie Mary would look like emerging foolishly from her grave wondering where Jimmy was and what happened to the deeds and the money. Like the solitary bones mixed up with wood and earth and nettle roots, she thought. Auntie Mary would not be a pretty sight on that day. But she never was. And then she wondered what her father's name was and whether he was dead or alive.

FOUR

'Patricia is a lovely name,' Mrs Casey said. 'It is the feminine form of St Patrick's name. In Latin he would be Patricius and if he was a girl he would be Patricia. So you're called after St Patrick.' She held a slice of toast between her finger and thumb, a bubble of butter developing on the underside, and when she was finished speaking she put it in her mouth and bit part of it off. She put the rest back on her plate and picked up the cup of frothy milk-coffee. She swallowed some and continued to chew the toast. 'Wasn't the bishop lovely?' she asked, her words thick with doughy toast. 'He always gives a great sermon.'

Josephine shuffled Baby Jean on to her other knee and tried to get her to eat a spoon of cornflakes. She made sucking sounds with her lips and, once or twice, furtively, brushed her fingers lightly against her cheek, marvelling at the translucent beauty of the baby's skin. She had boiled milk and then cooled it. She had sprinkled sugar on the bowl of cornflakes and then poured the warm milk over it. She had allowed the wrinkled golden flakes to soak and straighten out so that they looked like limp petals. When the baby took the spoonful Josephine brought her face close and nuzzled her, the sullen face wrinkling into a smile. 'That's my girl.' Another spoonful.

Then she said: 'He had a huge car. The bishop had.'

The windscreen was darkened so that no one could see inside, who was in there or what was going on. Bishops liked their mystery, she supposed, and their privacy. They like to emerge into the sunlight nodding and waving to small crowds, people to come forwards and kiss their rings. Never kiss a hand, Auntie Mary used to say. You never know what it's been shaking.

Mrs Casey laughed. 'You should see the palace.' Josephine saw a picture of a castle from Disney, a shambles of turrets and battlements. If you wish upon a star, makes no difference who you are. 'Why does a bishop have a palace?' she asked.

'That's only the word for it,' Mrs Casey said. 'It's just a very big house.' She smiled indulgently at Josephine. 'You're such an innocent,' she said. 'Sure you've never been anywhere. What am I going to do with you at all?'

'I'm going to travel,' Josephine said. 'When I'm big. To broaden my mind.' Travel Broadens the Mind: an article in *Woman's Way*. It expands horizons, the article said. It brings new experiences. Josephine felt she would like new experiences in time, but not immediately. She had recently made her confirmation and had been disappointed by the effect. She felt none of the things that first the master, then the curate and finally the bishop said she would feel. She did not feel stronger, or better able to resist temptation, or closer to God but she had been sitting in the second row from the front and all around her were the girls she had grown up with and they were just children whereas she was already working. Now they might remember the things they had called her, and her mother, and they might repent.

Dr Casey's Cortina came up the drive. Its wheels seemed to press weightily on the pebbles, purposeful, never fast. When it stopped they saw that he had a patient in the back seat. The patient was doubled over. Dr Casey got out and shortly they heard him on the telephone in the front hall. While he spoke Mrs Casey and Josephine stared at the car but the patient did not straighten up. The kitchen door opened and Dr Casey came in.

'Would you believe that?' he said. 'The so and sos won't send the ambulance. They said could I drive him up. I said what about my other patients. Supposing there was another emergency. Supposing I had a brain haemorrhage or a car accident.'

'What is it Peter?'

'Appendicitis,' he said. 'Any chance of a cup of tea. The bitch said she'd ring me back in ten minutes.'

'Josephine, put on the kettle. Peter, we should invite him in.'

Dr Casey said bitch again and shook his head. Mrs Casey went out to the car and spoke to the patient. Josephine noticed the slight twist of her body that had been caused by the osteomyelitis. 'My own father was a doctor,' she told Josephine once, 'and he brought it home with him.' Josephine imagined the doctor delivering up a gift to his daughter after work one evening, something shapeless, pretty on the outside but dirty on the inside. When she opened it, she had osteomyelitis. The word pleased Josephine, the rhythm of it, the hissing sound. Dr Casey said you rarely saw it bad nowadays. Mrs Casey had been sick for a long time and then she got better but it left her with a slight twist, almost unnoticeable. It made her look human, attractive, like a slight turn in the eye. Josephine liked it. 'Dirt causes disease,' Mrs Casey said once. Her own blonde hair was always shining. Her clothes perfect.

The patient straightened up and got slowly out of the car. Josephine saw that it was the man with the oiled hair who had asked her for a kiss in the graveyard. He walked stiffly, one hand on his right side as though he were suppressing something live and volatile, as though a small vicious animal might emerge from his underclothing and savage him at any moment. He came into the kitchen and sat at the table, bending awkwardly from the waist. Mrs Casey asked him if he would take a cup of tea or coffee. He shook his head. When he saw Josephine he looked surprised but he didn't say anything. Then he looked down at the child and winked at it: the child did not respond.

Dr Casey drank his cup of tea standing. He looked tired but his eyes were alert, fiery even, the anger of his exchange with the hospital still burning. His stethoscope curled out of the pocket of his jacket where he often kept it, the head gleaming against the greenish tweed like a flat steel mushroom. He made desultory conversation with the man, mostly about the harvest, which promised to be a good one if the rain held off. The man seemed to find it difficult to sustain a train of thought. He looked distracted and uneasy, changing his sitting posture frequently. The doctor rocked back and forth on his heels, balancing the cup and saucer in the flat of his left palm as though trying to prove that he could do it. Then the phone rang and he went out to the hall. His voice rumbled at them, sounding off the oak floor-boards, the high empty staircase, the stairs with the strip of carpet held in place with brass stair-rods.

Mrs Casey picked up her coat from the chair she had thrown it on and said that she'd had enough, was going for a drive and wouldn't be back until dinner-time. 'If the doctor is looking for me tell him I'm not anywhere, just driving. I can't be reached for a few hours. Peace and quiet,' she said turning to the patient. 'That's what I crave. Peace and quiet out of this place. Away from the telephone and people with . . . complaints.'

The man nodded uncomfortably. 'That must be desperate,' he said.

'Night and day, there's never a quiet hour.'

'I'd say that all right.'

She turned to Josephine. 'Take her for a walk if the rain holds off,' she said. 'And mind you keep her warm.'

'I will Mrs Casey.'

'Don't let her eat blackberries this time. They're full of maggots.'

'I won't.'

'And she's not to play with the cat.'

'I can't keep her away from that cat,' Josephine said.

'She'll get her allergy again. She'll inhale those hairs.'

'I know, Mrs Casey, but she won't keep away from the cat.'

Mrs Casey made a disapproving face and left. Josephine heard her car rippling down the gravel and then changing gears and revving on the main road. Mrs Casey's driving was erratic, full of shunts and partially engaged gears, high revving, jerky stops and starts. It was part of her personality. Josephine was pleased that Mrs Casey hardly ever wanted to hold Baby Jean. She liked dressing her up and changing her and patting her back when she had wind. Sometimes she thought it was all a dream, or that it was some kind of game. She could hardly believe she had been given this child to mind. But she took it very seriously and when she had time she practised everything on her own doll. Mrs Casey didn't enjoy any of those things. She was like Josephine's mother in that.

Josephine spoke to Baby Jean who was playing with the spoon in the bowl of cornflakes. She was thinking: that child is going to spill everything. What would the man think? She looked at him and saw that his face was yellow and strained and shiny like patent leather. She caught the rank full smell of sweat and something else. A man-smell. She knew it. It was the smell of her childhood. His hair was still oiled though now it was coarse and towy looking, stranded rope. His elbows rested on his knees, both of his hands were pressed against his stomach and his breathing was short and noisy. She saw that he was wearing a workman's trousers and jacket and a pair of heavy boots. She supposed that the tweed jacket he wore in the graveyard was only for funerals or special occasions.

'Have you still got the lighter?' she asked. He looked at her, surprised. 'I'd say you don't want the kiss now.' He groaned and looked away.

'Like in the pictures. With the mouth open. I'd give it to you now if you had the lighter.'

'Jesus Christ,' he said. He looked sideways at her and nodded his head quickly, almost a flick, half winking an eye at the same time. 'You're game all right, fair dues.'

'Have you it?'

'Take it!' He drew one hand away from his side and took the lighter out of his pocket. He threw it on the table. 'Keep the bastard.' He put his hand back to his side.

'What ails you?'

'Appendix he says.' They heard the doctor's angry voice arguing about a bed. They listened together for a time.

'Only sometimes he can't get people in,' she said. 'And they never want to send the ambulance out this far unless it's life and death.'

'Shut up will you.'

Josephine looked at his grey face, the way he held his hand low on his stomach, pressing on it as though he were holding his innards in place. She put her hand down on the lighter and felt its cold form against her palm. She closed her hand quickly and put the lighter in her pocket.

'Are you going to die?'

'Shut up will you. For Chris'sake shut up.'

'I was only asking.' The man twisted uneasily. His hand circled low on his stomach, his breathing coarser now. Josephine could hear it coming through his mouth where the lower lip hung down like open trousers. There was something nasal in it too, a faint whistle. 'I found my Auntie Mary dead.' He looked bleakly at her, not understanding. That she was familiar with death. That she felt at home in its presence. She saw that he had black hair in his nose, tendrils twisting out into the air, black spiders clinging to the underside of the tip. And his lower face was pitted with pores, each capped with a tiny black spot, and with the small coarse black hair of his beard, shaved but not recently.

Dr Casey came back in. He was smiling and rubbing his hands together. 'I put the fear of God in them Dick. Hah? That old whoor, I know her well. I did my intern up there. Christ, you'd swear she was paying for the petrol out of her own pocket. Anyway, they're sending the ambulance. It'll be here in half an hour. I got you a bed under Lawton. I'll give you a letter for him.'

The news seemed to cheer the man. When Dr Casey went out again he straightened up and winked at Josephine. 'Is there a cuppa?' he asked. 'Maybe I'd hold down a drop.' Josephine got a cup and poured for him. Baby Jean climbed under the table and began to talk to herself quietly. 'Jaze that's a contented child,' the man said. He said, 'I puked me guts out last night. If I did it once I did it ten times. I thought it was bad porter. A bad pint. Only for the mother sending,' he jerked his thumb in the direction of the hall, 'I'd be dead now.' She noticed that he put three spoons of sugar into his tea. His spoon clattered in the cup.

'So you have a mother?'

'Jaze,' the man said, 'everyone have a mother. Anyone could be your father but you only have the one mother.'

'She's still alive so.'

'Well, I'm not keeping the corpse on the kitchen table am I?'

'I thought you were too old,' Josephine said.

He swallowed a quick noisy gulp and then stopped, the cup suspended between his lips and the saucer. He seemed to be anticipating something, a quizzical look in his face. After a moment he grunted and took a second swallow. He put the cup down.

'So far so good,' he said. 'Tell us, is it hard to manage the young wan?'

Josephine smiled. 'She's nearly as good as mine,' she said. But only Susan was really hers. Susan never complained, never got dirty, never needed to be handed to someone else. Susan's love was complete and unconditional. Josephine loved to bathe and clean her, dress her, cuddle and care for her. She looked now at Baby Jean and wished that she was entirely her own to be loved and cared for like the doll.

'Mrs Casey is hardly ever in. I do everything for her. I dress her up and I keep her clean. I'm allowed to give her her bath. Mrs Casey likes me to play with her. She says it keeps her mind active. I'm allowed to go out for a walk with her.' Baby Jean in the pram, a serene face above the pale pink blankets, object of admiration to passers-by – 'Oh she's gorgeous! How old is she? Can I hold her?'

'What about nights?'

'I'm in charge all night,' Josephine said.

'Do she keep you awake?'

Josephine shook her head. 'She sleeps like a doll.' A foxy look came into her eyes. 'I can make her do anything I want.'

'What about the cat so? You told herself you couldn't keep her away from the cat.'

'That's all my eye,' Josephine said. 'I only said that. She never goes near the cat. I was only saying it.'

'Which room are you in?' the man asked, a look of comical cunning rippling over his face, a cloud's shadow on a weathered rock.

'The one at the back, over the back kitchen,' she said. 'The one with the red curtains.'

'Are you ever lonesome?' Suddenly he doubled over again, his hands locked across his stomach. 'Ah Jesus,' he said. His head touched the saucer and the cup tipped sideways, tea flooding the table. The cup rolled over the edge and broke into three pieces on the floor. 'Look what you did!' Josephine scolded. She rushed over to the sink and squeezed out a cloth. She mopped the tea on the table. Suddenly the baby started to cry.

'The young wan is cut,' the man said, looking sideways at the underside of the table. The sweat was water on his face now, a clear stream. The smell was strong.

Josephine picked her up and looked at the tiny hand. A half-inch slit reddened in the palm. The baby was wailing and twisting spasmodically. 'You stupid brat!' Josephine said.

'She's in the right place anyway,' the man gasped. Josephine thought he was laughing. 'Is there a doctor in the house!' he said and gasped again.

Now the baby was kicking and calling for her daddy. 'I'll be murdered,' Josephine said. 'Mrs Casey'll slaughter me.'

'Why don't you get the doc to bandage her?' the man asked.

Josephine picked up the tea-towel and wrapped it tightly around the baby's hand. 'Pick up the cup after yourself,' she said. She opened the back door and pulled a large blue pram out of the porch. She put the baby into it and threw two blankets over it. 'Good luck so,' she said, and pushed the pram out through the back door into the sunlight.

She pushed the pram before her through the clutching gravel of the drive. Baby Jean wore a pink frilled dress with a lace collar. Her face was pale with red spots. Her mouth was open and short stifled wails came from it. At first Josephine tried to keep her hands inside the blankets so that the blood would not be seen but then she worried that the blood would dirty the lovely dress. She took the hand out and knotted the tea-towel and tried to arrange the baby's hands so as to avoid staining the blankets but the hands would not stay still. She wondered what Mrs Casey would say. Jean was always so clean and Mrs Casey liked things in their right places and kept well. She walked as far as a narrow lane and turned into it. Then she lifted the baby out and put it on her left shoulder. 'There there, pet,' she said, tapping her back lightly. 'Josephine will make it all better. There now.' She walked up and down in the shadow of the hawthorns soothing the child. 'Poor Baby Jean,' she said. 'My poor little Baby Jean.'

FIVE

The horn bayed once in the icy clarity of the night. Josephine started as though shocked. She looked out and saw the minibus rumbling quietly at the gate, the driver hunched over the wheel in the loom of the headlights. 'I'm off now, Susan,' she said. 'Be good.' She took the doll from the bed and held her high, like a mother hoisting a child above her head. Light came through the sallow head so that it looked like she was lit from within, electrifying her hair and the diaphanous material of her dress. Then she brought her face down and kissed it, and placed the doll on the bed slightly propped against the pillow. 'I'll tell you all about it when I get back,' she said. 'Sleep well.' She went downstairs and Mrs Casey met her in the hall with her anorak. She smiled and nodded her head in the direction of the front door. 'That's them,' she said.

'I know.'

Mrs Casey said that she looked like the real thing. Then she sang a snatch of a song: 'Puttin' on the agony, puttin' on the style . . . You're going to be popular tonight, Josephine.'

She walked slowly round her, dusted off her shoulders, adjusted the neck of her blouse. Josephine bore it all, trembling like a nervous horse.

'Nervous?'

Josephine's stomach churned uncomfortably. She wondered whether she would need to go to the toilet again before going out. 'A bit.'

Mrs Casey smiled again. 'I remember my first time.'

Josephine pulled on the anorak and straightened her hair in the mirror. She opened the front door.

'Be good now,' Mrs Casey said. 'Don't do anything I wouldn't do.'

Josephine ran down the drive to the minibus. The driver opened the door and she climbed up on to the front seat. She could hear a subdued murmur from the back of the bus. 'How's she cuttin'?' the driver said.

'Grand.'

'Right,' the driver said. He put the bus in gear and pulled out. 'Ten bob or fifty pee, whichever you call it.' Josephine handed him the coins. 'Have mon will travel,' the driver said. Josephine laughed.

'Your man on the telly,' the driver said. 'What's his name. I can't remember it. Have gun will travel he says.'

Someone started to sing. 'Many homes are filled with sorrow and with sadness, many hearts are filled with anguish and with pain . . .' The others joined in, their voices rising above the rumble of the engine. Josephine turned round and saw that the singer was a girl her own age, recognised her from school. She sang with her eyes closed, nodding her head emphatically at the end of each line. When she finished they all clapped. A boy struck up a song she had never heard. 'An old man came courting me, hey ding dorum da, an old man came courting me, me being young, an old man came courting me, damn nearly smothered me, maids when you're young never wed an old man.' The chorus was raucous. As the song became more suggestive they shouted encouragement to him and his voice became throaty. The driver laughed loudly and slapped his hand on the wheel. When the boy finished the driver turned to Josephine and said, 'Jaze the hard man, hah? Would you doubt him?'

The minibus swung into a carpark and the headlights illuminated what looked like an enormous barn. 'All change at Limerick Junction,' the driver said, turning in his seat to wink at them. 'See you after,' they all said and the driver said they might or they might not. 'Maybe I'll click myself,' he shouted after them. But when they had all spilled out laughing and chattering Josephine saw him lean back in his seat and rub his eyes, and she heard the faint sound of music played on a radio underscored by static.

The boys and girls separated in the queue. A huge sign attached to the upper rim of the hall said ATLANTIC BALLROOM. Some of the bulbs were gone and others flickered nervously. A man with a long pointed jaw and hollow eyes tore tickets off a thick red roll. 'Move along now. Next.' He slapped the ticket on the little wooden tray. 'Next.'

Inside, the crowd was standing about on the floor or leaning against the mineral bar. 'There'll be no drink, Grace,' Dr Casey told his wife. 'It's a mineral licence only.' But as Josephine watched she saw a boy take a flat whiskey bottle from his jacket pocket and drink surreptitiously from it. He wiped his lips with his sleeve and looked around to see who was watching. He saw Josephine and winked at her. There was no air and Josephine felt her breathing quicken. She smelled perfume, hair-oil, sweat, old clothes. The ladies' was a brief respite, cold air from windows that opened high over their heads on worm-action gears, sweetened by perfume and urine. A clatter of girls putting on lipstick and powder, touching up blushes and darkening eyeliner. Suggestive talk. Josephine locked herself in a cubicle for five minutes, allowing her breathing to steady, studying the cracked blue Formica of the door. The pattern reminded her of the varicosed mottling of Auntie Mary's legs. Her wooden legs, she used to call them. But they weren't wood and sometimes the veins would bubble up below the skin and spread dark stains in the deltas and then Auntie Mary would moan and complain and drink more tonic wine.

When she returned to the hall the band was on stage arranging the instruments and microphones. The front of one of the drums had the band's name in fancy scrollwork: the Hi-Rollers. They wore shiny blood-coloured jackets with a gold edging on the lapels. The man who was arranging the microphones tapped each one and said one-two-one-two into each in turn. He fiddled with something halfway down each stand and adjusted the height. Suddenly the drummer began to rattle out a soft beat. The drums were a low-pitched insistent rattle and every now and then he touched the cymbals and their bright metallic laughter rippled through the hall.

The crowd gradually turned to face them. Lemonade bottles were upended and drained. When the bandleader announced that they would begin with the ancient 'Hucklebuck' there was a ripple of applause shot through with shouts of derision. The drummer commenced the beat. The first instrument to join him was a saxophone. A man with an electric guitar was playing too but Josephine could not distinguish the sound he was making. Her nervousness was gone now. Instead she was absorbed in watching the performance on stage. By the time the round-faced singer was leaning into the microphone singing with an imitation American accent, her foot was tapping and her hips were swinging a little. She was standing on the edge of the dance-floor among a group of about twenty girls. The floor was crowded and she could not see where anyone else could fit, but every few seconds a boy would emerge from the throng and speak to one of the girls. Then they would walk away together and be swallowed up.

The band went straight into the next tune without a pause. The dancers looked briefly surprised and then continued their jumbled movements. Josephine noticed that there were no steps to these dances, although one of the older couples was doing the twist, bending their knees progressively and swivelling wildly, balanced on the balls of their feet. The climax of the twist came when the couple were squatting down almost on their haunches, their arms outstretched, swivelling frenetically. Then they rose gradually again. Sometimes they twisted on one leg with the other bent at the knee and sticking it out at a crazy angle. It looked comical and she laughed and felt herself swivelling too. The other dancers seemed to ignore each other, weaving or swaying without even catching each other's eyes. It did not seem very intimate.

A boy came up to her and asked her if she would like to dance. Suddenly terrified again she said she would. He led her on to the dance-floor and when the band struck up a slow tune he put his two hands around her waist and started to move gently. The movement seemed directionless to Josephine, but she allowed herself to be led by it. The boy asked her did she come often and when she said it was her first time he looked surprised.

'I'm here every Saturday,' he said. 'But when I get to college it'll be all discos. There's no more bands up in college now, so my brother told me. He says it's all rubbish, the bands. What do you think of them?'

Josephine said she thought they were great. He smiled and wrinkled up his face. 'Do you like Rory Gallagher?' he asked and she said she didn't know him. The boy laughed. 'That's a good one,' he said. After a time he put his cheek beside her ear and they danced in silence. When the tune ended he said, 'Thanks very much. See you later.' She walked off and he went in another direction. Later she saw him dancing with the girl who sang the song on the minibus. She was conscious of a faint sense of disappointment.

At about midnight he came back. 'Will you give me a dance?' he said. His face was white and his eyes were red and stood out on the white like berries in snow. There were beads of sweat on his forehead. Josephine had danced only twice more and her feet were sore from standing around, but she agreed. The bandleader was standing at the microphone. 'We're gonna finish off with a couple of slow numbers for all you last-chancers,' he said. He named the two songs and said, 'It's been great to be here again. We'll be in the Top Hat next Saturday night. In the meantime, be good and if you can't be good be careful.' The guitarist stepped forwards to the front of the stage and with a look of intense concentration began to pick out a set of low resonant notes. After a time the singer took the stand of the microphone in his hand and tilted the whole thing towards him. 'There is a house in New Orleans,' he sang, 'They call the

Rising Sun. It's been the ruin of many a poor boy, Oh Lord I know I'm one.' The whole crowd moved in a slow urgent rhythm, unified by the music, a single animal. The air was sweating, water dripping from the ceiling, running on the patches of elaborate wallpaper that decorated niches around the hall, the smell of sweat was the air itself. Overhead light splintered off a ball coated with glass shreds throwing strange fragments of colour on everything. The faces that reeled slowly past Josephine had a dreamlike appearance, birthmarked by the scraps of light. Many of the girls had their heads on the shoulders or chests of their boys. Their arms were around each other. Some of them moved their hands slowly over each other's backs, even down to the buttocks.

The boy held her close so that her movements had to match his exactly. She could feel his upper thighs moving against hers and she was forced to arch backwards slightly in order to be able to move. His hands were in the small of her back. After a time she found it easier to put her head on his shoulder and when she did he began to move his hands. She could feel them brushing her broad white leather belt and at other times he seemed to be rubbing her shoulder-blades. As the band moved into the second song he lifted her head up and kissed her. He kissed her on the lips and she felt his tongue pushing in. She opened her mouth and he began to move his face on hers. She knew it was the same kind of kiss the man with oiled hair had wanted. His tongue in her mouth was rasping, a small animal looking for a bolt-hole. After a time he stopped and she put her head back on his shoulder. When the band stopped playing they both clapped and while the rest of the crowd called for an encore he said, 'Will you come outside?'

A full grey moon was up and now she could see that the dance-hall was on the edge of a series of sand dunes. The boy led her between the mounds and she felt the coarse marram scratching at her thighs. 'Are you in school?' the boy asked.

She said that she was working.

'Where?'

She said that she was a housekeeper for a doctor.

'Cushy,' he said. 'I'm doing the Leaving. I can't wait to get it over.'

She asked him what he was going to do after the Leaving. 'I'm going to England,' he said. He said it angrily. 'I can't wait to get on that bloody boat.'

'I thought you said college?' It's all discos now in college he had said. She remembered it.

'That's what my folks think too. Well, I'm not.'

'Why?'

They had twisted and turned through several layers of dunes. Once or twice she had seen the dark shapes of other couples standing or lying in the marram. They made no sound.

'Ach, I'm sick of books,' he said. 'My father wants me to be a teacher or something but I don't care.' He began to imitate a deep, thickly accented voice: 'Son get your degree first, that way you'll have something behind you. You can drop out after that for all you're worth. Get the bit of paper first.'

They stopped suddenly and he put his arms around her again. 'I like you,' he said. She smiled. 'I mean it. The rest of them in there,' he nodded his head at one of the dunes, 'they're all the same.' She heard the scorn in his voice. 'They're all shagging lousers.' He looked into her face and seemed to be studying it. He tilted his head to one side and smiled gently. 'You have lovely eyes.'

He kissed her again, gently at first, then with more urgency. His hands moved up and down her back. After a time one hand working inside her blouse, his fingers rippling on her spine. Then his second hand began to move upwards. When it encountered her bra strap it stopped for a time, an insect encountering an obstacle. He stopped kissing and hugged her instead. Then he sat her down in the sand.

'That's some moon,' he said. They looked up at it together for a time, the blank unmoved face. Then his hand came up under the front of her blouse. Before she had time to notice he had lifted the cups of her bra up on to her upper chest and held one of her breasts in his hand. 'Oh,' she said. He looked at her and darted his face on to hers. He pushed his tongue into her mouth as though to stop her from saying anything. At the same time he began to massage her nipple. She pulled her face away. 'Stop that,' she said. He chuckled but continued to rub. She pushed his hand away and pulled down the bra again. He said, 'You really are the best-looking girl in the place.'

'Don't do that any more,' she said.

'Outside?' he asked. He put his hand on her blouse outside the bra. Again he began to rub her breast. It was the same breast. He kissed her and leaned against her so that she tilted backwards into the sand. She closed her eyes, hearing the balance click in her head, then opened them again. The moon greyed the darkness. He leaned over her, his upper body on hers. He put one leg on her thigh. Then she was aware that he was fumbling with the belt of her jeans. She pushed him away and sat up. 'The bus'll be gone,' she said. Sea air was rustling in the sand, cool on her face. She could hear the distant collapse of waves on wet sand.

'The band is still playing,' he said. 'They always do three or four encores. Listen.' Faintly across the dunes came the rhythm of a song she didn't know, a repetitive sibilant thrusting rhythm. 'They'll be ten minutes yet.'

'I'm going.' She stood up and tucked her blouse into her jeans.

'You're joking.'

'I am not.'

He stood up and caught her arms. He kissed her hard and then looked into her face. 'You're not interested, are you?'

She shook her head.

'You're fucking frigid, that's what you are.'

55

'I am not.' She walked back the way they came, weaving between the clumps of marram, following the thin grey line of sand that wound in and out among islands of grass, dunes, patches of small scrub. They had to cross a thin stream and she couldn't remember meeting it before. Was she lost? Once she heard moaning from the shadows and wondered if it was someone who wanted to escape but couldn't. The boy caught up with her after a time and walked beside her with short rapid steps. Sometimes, when the path narrowed he had to walk higher than her along the edge of a dune. At times his feet seemed to be moving in slow motion, going away from him into the softer sand.

'Look,' he said, 'I really like you. I was a bit fast all right. Look, hold on a bit.' She increased her pace. 'Look fuck it. I thought you were interested. I wasn't going to rape you.'

The minibus was ahead of her in a pool of shadow. It was about half full. Even though the door was closed she could hear the hubbub of voices and the soft music from inside. The band had stopped playing and there were clusters of people standing here and there, occasional couples in passionate embraces. Two men were arguing in loud voices, one holding a black pint bottle and swigging out of it occasionally. He swayed as he talked.

When he saw the minibus the boy caught her arm and spun her around. 'You're the first one ever did that to me,' he said. 'I won't forget it.'

'Let me go will you.'

'You're a frigid bitch, that's what you are. I'll spread the word about that. It's the last time you'll ever get danced.'

'Who cares.'

'Well Jesus Christ. Just my luck to pick the only virgin in the place.' He let go of her hand and spun away. 'You dirty bitch, you wasted my night,' he said without turning around.

The driver played an English radio station all the way home, humming the tunes and chuckling at the presenter's quips. He named every song and every band before the presenter. 'Lindisfarne,' he would say. 'Fog on the Tyne'. Josephine watched him carefully. 'How do you do that?' she said. The driver laughed. 'That's what gets everyone,' he said. 'How do I do it?' He shrugged his shoulders and moved a little in his seat. 'You'd want to be years at it,' he said. The news came on, a clipped English voice talking about the latest fuss in the House of Commons, a near miss over Heathrow, the finding of a child's body on a common near London, the results of a Test Match and gossip about a tennis star. Josephine thought of the baby's room in Dr Casey's house. Jean would be asleep in her white night-dress, her legs splayed, her hair disordered on the pillow. Josephine thought of the dribble of mucus that came from her mouth and soiled the white pillow. There was always something, she thought, no such thing as the perfect picture. There was always a stain. Except for Susan. She thought of how she cared for Susan – the bathing, washing her clothes, combing her beautiful blonde hair. And Susan's face looked up at her from her reverie with unquestioning love, the apple-cheeks bruised by a smile, the eyes open and trusting or with long lashes splayed over pale skin. And Susan slept by her side at night, the tiny body thrust into hers, her own baby, her own love, never-changing, always perfect.

She dozed in the minibus's warmth, Susan and Jean drifting in and out of her dreams, a bold child with a plain dead face, a pretty doll with apple cheeks. Once, in the dream, Jean came to her from the sea and Josephine recognised that she was frozen, coming from the blue of an icy deep, hands hooked like claws. She tried to catch at her waist, fumbled with her belt and zip, the way the boy had done. 'I really like you,' she was saying. She was Uncle Jimmy coming to straighten her out, but he would fail as he had always failed before. 'You're dead,' she told him. 'You're never coming back.' She woke with a start as the minibus came through the village and looked around, but no one seemed to have noticed that she was asleep. The people in the bus were mostly silent. In the very back a couple kissed and murmured. When the minibus stopped at Dr Casey's house the driver leaned past Josephine and opened her door. 'See you next week love,' he said.

'Yeah. Be seeing you,' she said.

SIX

'Stop calling her Baby Jean,' Mrs Casey said sharply. 'She's four now. She'll be in school in September.'

Josephine said she was sorry. It was a habit.

'Go easy on her Grace,' Dr Casey said. 'It's a term of affection.' He hummed happily and steered with one hand, the other on the gear-shift. 'Did you pack the wine?'

'Josephine did.'

'Good girl Josephine,' he said, turning round in the front seat and smiling at her. He winked at Baby Jean. 'How's my pet?'

He started to tell them about an opportunity to buy a share in a racehorse, but suddenly the broad road ended and in the narrow twisting lane that passed for a highway they were trapped behind a convoy of pea-harvesters, pale green and ungainly, like mechanical armadillos.

'What's that?' Jean asked.

'Jesus!' Mrs Casey said. 'I thought she was asleep.'

'A pea-harvester,' Dr Casey said. 'For harvesting peas.'

He pulled out on a wider patch and overtook one of them and now they were trapped between two. The driver of the harvester behind them glared down. He appeared to be singing, his mouth opening and closing like a fish's. They were surrounded by the clatter of the machines. Cars whizzed by on the other side of the road, appearing suddenly from the harvester in front, vanishing quickly behind, disconnected, isolated events. On their own side the ditches crawled by, punctuated occasionally by gates, by-roads or houses. Once they overtook a cyclist labouring on a hill. He was laden with camping gear. He wore round glasses and skin-tight shorts, an exotic in the nondescript countryside. 'A visitor,' was Dr Casey's judgement. 'A German probably. I wonder where he's off to?'

The cyclist's shorts reminded her of the long-legged cotton drawers that Susan wore – old-fashioned and always out-of-season looking. Yet she would not change them, although she had remade and repaired the dress, the cardigan and the socks. 'I'm going to have to take the dress away for repairs,' she would tell Susan. 'You can have a bath while I'm stitching it.' She would let Susan float in the basin, talking quietly about the kind of day she had or the latest gossip, a patchwork of stories, dreams and endearments, her fingers picking out the tiny stitches, following where possible the holes that previous needles had pricked. 'My baby,' she would call her while she talked, or 'My love'. Or 'My Susan.' Later she would hold the body down, feeling the doll's failing buoyancy, watching the bubbles rise from leg and arm joints and the place where the neck was inserted in the torso. After a time Susan would cease to struggle against the invading water. Her body would sink – never entirely because there was always some air trapped in the shell – and the head would float clear. The head was a closed unit that never let water in except through the eyes, and she was careful never to immerse the eyes. Susan's head would bob happily, rotating this way and that in the mysterious currents and wavelets of the basin. Afterwards Josephine would drain away the water and clean her down with a soft cloth, wiping imaginary dust from her arms, her face, her pudgy chest and the flat sexless place between her legs. Look what the nice man brought you. And it was Susan.

'We're never going to get there at this rate,' Mrs Casey said. 'We'd be quicker walking.'

'Keep your hair on,' Dr Casey said. 'It won't run away. The day is our own.'

'Finally,' she said. 'One day in two years.'

'Now that's an exaggeration, Grace, and you know it isn't easy to get a locum. And they like to talk to their own doctor. They don't like strangers.'

'It isn't easy to give up the money you mean.' She raised her hand towards the windshield and made a smoothing pinching gesture with her thumb and index finger. He looked at it with distaste. His hands whitened on the wheel.

'Well someone has to make it,' he said. 'You certainly know how to spend it, anyway.'

She laughed. She turned in her seat, all smiles now. 'How's my Jeanie?' she said. She reached back and patted her face. 'Won't be long now.'

'Is there going to be climbing trees?' Jean said.

'Plenty,' Josephine said.

'Don't go destroying your clothes,' Mrs Casey said.

'Keep an eye on her,' Dr Casey told Josephine. 'Don't let her get up too far.'

They swung through a gateway and past a signpost that said Killacurry Forest Park, the tyres pounding and hammering over the rough road. Josephine saw dark green trees crowded too close together, reaching desperately upwards, a dense brown carpet that could have been coarse sackcloth. In the foreground sunlight gleamed on flinty gravel, and a scatter of papers and Coke bottles surrounded an overfull rubbish bin. There were log picnic tables at intervals around the carpark, a haughty crow on one of them picking at something grey. When the car stopped there was a sudden absolute silence.

'First things first,' Dr Casey said. 'Grub.' He opened the door and stretched himself. He took the *Irish Independent* from the dashboard and went to sit on a picnic bench. He looked around him for a moment with evident satisfaction, then he shook the newspaper out and began to read. Josephine opened the boot and lifted the picnic basket. She felt the dead weight of the wine bottle and wondered what it tasted like. She could smell the chicken, still warm from the oven. Her mouth watered.

Mrs Casey sat in the car glaring at her husband.

Jean walked tentatively towards the nearest tree then turned around and walked back again. The crow swooped lazily from the table and then rose into the blue air above the trees. The grey thing was gone.

Josephine watched insects drifting lazily in the clearing. Infused with sunlight against the darker shadows of the wood they seemed to be lit from the inside. The smell of heat and mould reminded her of home – stale turf, alcohol, yesterday's sweat – heady and foetid at the same time. Where she stood a mob of brown toadstools protruded from the rank soil. She heard the distant rumble of voices at the picnic table and, further away, the groaning and clattering of harvesters at work. She heard Jean's uneasy breathing, her feet shuffling among pine needles, the occasional crack of a stick.

Hide and seek.

She was good at hide and seek.

The child came into view and Josephine watched her totter uncertainly into the light. She lifted and placed her feet with cartoon exaggeration, tiptoeing. She looked slowly to each side, registering only shadows, trees, pine-needles. She smiled. She dashed across the clearing, flashing in and out of sunlight and straight into Josephine's arms. She screamed.

'Got you!' Josephine shouted. She swung the child into the air, laughing into her face. Terror changed to pleasure. 'Again!' the child shouted. 'Play again Josephine!'

Josephine set her down on the soft brown carpet. 'I'm closing my eyes,' she said. 'I'm counting.' She began a slow count from twenty down. Jean looked from side to side, panicked, then rushed away into the shadows. Josephine counted on. 'Three, two, one, nought. Watch out! Here comes the bogeyman.'

She stepped back into the shadows and waited patiently. The air hung heavy around her. After a time she distinguished the sound of something moving in the forest. She set off at an angle to the clearing, stepping lightly, silently. Every few paces she stopped again and listened.

'I hear you,' she whispered.

Like holding her breath in bed when she was a child. Like hearing the sounds from the kitchen, the scraping of chairs, footsteps, whispers, creaking bedsprings. Eventually, the pounding of her heart would become so loud it would sound like someone pounding against the wall of her room. Then she could hear nothing, drowning in noise. How was it that you could hear your own heart and not someone else's? She would have to breathe again. In a rush. Noisy air. It would be some time before she could hold her breath. Silence choked her.

She saw Baby Jean crouched behind a tree, watching the clearing. She crept up slowly, carefully. When she stood directly over her she reached down suddenly and pinched her back. The child screamed and jumped as though electrocuted. 'Here comes the bogeyman!' Josephine shouted gleefully. 'Got you again! You'll never be any good at hiding.'

Josephine lay on the rug staring up at the slowly accumulating clouds. Beside her, Jean slept with her thumb in her mouth, breathing sonorously and occasionally murmuring. Somewhere in the woods Dr and Mrs Casey rambled and argued. The picnic had not gone well. The heat of the day and the wine had given Mrs Casey a headache, which she blamed on her husband.

'You can't expect me to bring the dispensary with me everywhere I go, Grace,' Dr Casey had said, and she replied that she thought he was a doctor and why couldn't he cure a common headache. Dr Casey laughed and said he would tell them one he heard the other day.

'A fellow comes into the doctor with a bad cold,' he said. '"Can you give me something for it, doctor?" says he. "I can not," says the doctor, "but if you take a cold bath and stand in a draft with no clothes on you'll get pneumonia out of it and we can cure that."' The doctor laughed uproariously at his own joke. 'That's a good one all right,' he said. Josephine laughed too, although she could not see the humour in it. Mrs Casey stared at her husband and then chuckled.

'Not bad. Not bad at all,' she said. 'I get it.'

After that he had suggested a walk and they went off into the trees together, arguing about the wine.

Josephine rolled on to her side and looked at Baby Jean. Full of chicken, jam sandwiches and lemonade she had fallen asleep as naturally as if she were in her own bed. Now she was stirring a little. She rolled off her side and on to her back and kicked out slightly with one leg. Her left hand lay beside her, palm open and turned up, a gesture of trust. Josephine lightly brushed the hair out of her face and blew her a kiss. Then she got up and backed slowly away. When she reached the trees she stopped.

She stepped behind the tree and watched the child from its shadow. Her heart beat loudly and she found herself holding her breath again. She let it out slowly and quietly and forced herself to breathe.

After a time Jean's eyes were suddenly open. She looked up and saw that clouds were crossing the sun. She sat up and looked around. She gasped to see she was alone. She got to her feet and trotted over to the car. She looked inside. A cardigan was bunched on the passenger seat. A wasp was buzzing against the glass of the windscreen sure of its way home but unable to reach it. There was a ticking sound from the metal.

She surveyed the empty baking carpark, the picnic tables, the nearest trees drawing dark intensity from the heat. She gasped.

Jean had that look of seriousness small children have when they are trying to remember what they have been told to do in time of trouble. 'Stay where you are. Don't wander off.' She had heard it often enough. But now she made directly for the trees. She stared into the tent of shadows, studying. Strange shapes waited inside.

'Mammy! Josephine! Daddy!'

She did not cry.

She rushed through the pine-needles, veering left and right as the plantation allowed. When she realised she was lost she turned left and continued on a more direct path, as if such a simple alteration would bring her back again. After a time she began to shout. 'Mammy! Daddy! Josephine!' Then she sat down at the base of a tree, crushing a toadstool, and began to weep. She folded her arms across her knees and put her head down, huge sobs shaking her, her shoulders heaving.

Josephine Strane watched her for a time. She thought of Susan waiting silently at home, never disturbed no matter for how long she was alone, always serene, always welcoming. Then she stepped close behind her and said, 'Here comes the bogey-man!'

Jean gasped and jumped up. She threw herself into Josephine's arms. Josephine stroked her head, her shoulders. She hugged her. 'There there pet,' she said.

'I thought you were gone!'

'There now, pet,' Josephine said. 'You were lost, that's all. You got a fright.' There was something else there now, in the hot-mould smell, something sickly, warm and wet. Josephine sniffed and wondered what it was.

Dr Casey took the bends roughly and accelerated out of them in third gear until the engine was screaming. Once he overtook three cars and barely avoided a van that came at him around a blind bend. 'Take it easy Peter,' Mrs Casey said several times but he ignored her. He hummed snatches of songs and tapped a rhythm on the steering wheel.

The first thick drops of rain fell before they had left the forest park. Within two miles there was a summer downpour, the air turbid and breathless. 'A sub-tropical airflow,' the doctor said. 'That's what the forecast said. Warm moisture-laden air spreading northwards later in the day. A risk of isolated thundery showers. We got the best of it, I'd say.'

'Funny to think,' he said later, 'that this air is coming all the way up from Africa. Up through the Bay of Biscay, picking up water as it travels. I wonder what they thought of it down there.'

'I'll have to go down to see my mother at the weekend,' Mrs Casey said. 'She's not well at all.'

'Whatever you say, Grace,' Dr Casey said. 'I read somewhere that they pick up energy over the sea. Isn't that amazing? Then they hit the coast. Sure, Ireland is nearly all coast, when you think about it. By comparison with the continent.' He seemed pleased now. They had got the best of it.

'Her chest is very bad.'

'This kind of thing is bad for chest complaints all right,' Dr Casey said. 'I'll have all the asthmas and the emphysemas and bronchitises into me now tomorrow. I'll be lucky if I'm not called out tonight. Hay fever too.' He whistled through his teeth.

'I'll head off on Friday night.'

'Fine.'

Mrs Casey stared at the liquid world passing her window. 'Why did Jean wet herself?' she said.

'Now Grace,' Dr Casey said. 'That was all a misunderstanding.'

'I told you, Mrs Casey,' Josephine said. 'She got a bit of a fright. She thought we were all gone. She woke up and got a fright.'

'Why would she think that?'

'It was a call of nature,' Dr Casey said. 'Josephine has to go too. She thought Jean was asleep.'

'Anyway,' Mrs Casey said. 'I'll be back on Sunday night. I'll be back by eight or nine.'

Josephine held a story book for Jean, slowly turning the pages. Snow White slept in one, a face gleaming like delft on pale sheets. A dwarf stood at the foot of the bed wringing his hands, his comical face all twisted in sorrow. The window behind him showed a thick forest with ancient twisted trees and perhaps a faint suggestion of a prince riding towards them. Josephine knew that when she saw the next picture the prince would be actually there, standing by an elegant horse, smiling at the dwarfs, wearing a costume of green bedecked with jewels and a jewel-hilted sword.

She did not want to turn the page.

SEVEN

'Look at you child,' Mrs Casey exclaimed. 'Goodness, why didn't I notice it before?' Josephine saw a wildness in her, like a dog that had been locked up for too long. 'You're like a hungry sparrow, all bones and no feathers. What am I going to do with you at all? Here, get your coat. That bloody anorak, oh God, what will they say to you? That's the first thing that'll go anyway, that bloody anorak.' Josephine protested that she had the dinner to cook and Jean would be home from school. Mrs Casey waved her protest aside. 'For God's sake child, she won't be home until half three and the doctor is away all day. Strike while the iron is hot, that's my motto.'

'Look at you child,' Mrs Casey said again, staring at her in mock-horror. 'How long are you with us now? And you're still looking like a scarecrow.' Josephine couldn't believe that Mrs

Casey had not seen her before. She wondered if this was a trick. Then she thought Mrs Casey was always taking these humours, changing her mind about things, coming and going according to her own ways. *Figayries*, Auntie Mary used to call that kind of thing. *Taking figayries*. It was eleven miles to town. Since she came to Dr Casey's she had been away from the house, the little village, only once – to go to the dance. When Mrs Casey wanted her to go a second time she told her a story about heavy drinking and fights. 'Things have changed since my day,' she heard Mrs Casey say later. 'We just liked fun, good clean fun. Now it's all drink and drugs and fighting.'

'We'll have to get you dolled up.' Mrs Casey laughed at her own choice of phrase. 'Dolled up, that's it.' She began to croon 'My China Doll', swaying her hips and making caressing movements in the air in front of her. Then she laughed again, this time at Josephine's discomfort.

'I can't afford it,' Josephine said flatly, trying to look away although Mrs Casey came round to stand swaying and crooning in front of her again and she could not look away a second time without making it obvious. 'I have to save every penny,' she said. Because, she thought, I want to better myself: but she did not say it.

Mrs Casey stopped crooning and threw her hands into the air in an expression of abandonment. She went upstairs and in a moment could be heard opening drawers and closing them and cursing loudly. After a time she came downstairs. 'I have the bit of plastic,' she said. 'That famous bit of plastic.' She held up a Visa card. 'The sky's the limit on that.' She did a kind of shimmy at the foot of the stairs and grinned broadly. 'Come on girl, we're going to town.'

Josephine laughed nervously. 'I'll just put the roast in,' she said. She looked longingly at the large roll of beef lying on its side, a heavy drape of fat across its top, the nest of potatoes on either side. She thought of what they would smell like in an hour or two. 'I'll put them in on low,' she said. 'That way it'll be there when we get back.'

Mrs Casey maintained the wild humour all the way into town, her high spirits bubbling over every five minutes or so. 'Hey slowcoach!' she shouted at the driver of a battered Morris 1100 trailing a cloud of burnt oil, 'Pull over or roll over!' She grinned childishly and nudged Josephine whenever she thought she had made a particularly good remark. 'I saw that in a film,' she said at one stage. 'Last week.'

'When you were at your mother's?' Josephine said.

Mrs Casey stared tight-lipped at a red traffic light. When the light turned green she grinned again. 'It could've been the week before.' Mrs Casey's mother was not well and frequently called on her daughter's comfort. Mrs Casey would be away, usually for a weekend, and come back exhausted having been 'at the bedside twenty-four hours a day' as she put it. She would roll her eyes and shrug in a helpless way, conveying the impression that the old woman was irascible, domineering, hypochondriac.

Josephine pitied her these journeys, which seemed to take so much out of her. When she returned on a Sunday night with her little overnight suitcase in red leather and her small vanity case full of creams and Chanel and hairspray that she never travelled without, Josephine would say, 'I'll put the kettle on,' and when Mrs Casey went upstairs, Josephine would tiptoe up and leave the hot sweet tea on the edge of the bath where Mrs Casey would find it and be grateful for its restorative powers. She never wanted alcohol when she returned, although she liked to drink brandy as a night-cap usually. 'If I ever see another drink—' she said once, leaving the sentence unfinished, but causing Josephine to wonder whether her mother might also be alcoholic. She read a letter in *Woman's Realm* about a woman whose elderly mother was a difficult alcoholic and the letter-writer had made much of the pain she felt in divulging the information, even in admitting it to herself. The answer had advised openness, a self-help group, recourse to the excellent social services, and finally had sympathised. Josephine thought it was a wonderful letter and an equally wonderful and deep answer. She understood the problem because her mother always had bottles too, the smell of spirits in the air. The men brought them. And Auntie Mary drank Buckfast Tonic Wine. Made in Buckfast Abbey, the label said.

Mrs Casey parked the car crookedly, half of it on a double yellow line, and looked around like a dog assessing the chances of a rabbit. 'We'll start at Lacey's. They have a teenage section.'

They bought two new pairs of jeans at Lacey's, and a denim shirt with the stitching on the outside in coloured thread. The latest thing, according to Mrs Casey. 'I'm dropping for a coffee,' she told the assistant in Lacey's. But she insisted that they visit another shop, a department store, before they took a rest, Mrs Casey moving along with that attractive jaunty gait she had. Here she made Josephine try on a series of duffle coats. 'They suit your colour,' she said. She turned to the assistant. 'Look at those beautiful brown eyes. Doesn't that colour suit her perfectly?' The assistant looked at Josephine's eyes and agreed that the fawn-coloured coat she had on matched them to perfection. 'It's only gorgeous,' she said, looking at Josephine's eyes, not the coat. Irritated, Josephine tried to look away but when she glanced back the assistant was still studying her. 'I'll take it,' Mrs Casey said. She took out her card. 'You take Visa?' The assistant shook her head without looking away. 'I'll have to check.'

It turned out that the store did not take Visa and was, in fact, very reluctant to take a credit card at all. The manager was sent for and came down looking put upon. He was hostile at first, studying Josephine's old anorak with obvious disdain, but when Mrs Casey said, 'Well, why don't you just send the bill to Dr Peter Casey, Beechwood . . .' he became suddenly obsequious and anxious to please. 'Not at all, not at all,' he kept saying. 'I'm always saying we should start these cards, but sure there's no call for it around here.'

'Well,' Mrs Casey told him, 'get your finger out. Europe is here now. The EEC is going to turn this one horse country upside down.' The manager nodded his head vigorously and gazed at something in the shop window as though he were contemplating the arrival of a gang of European bandits who were hell-bent on ransacking his store.

In the end she wrote a cheque and the manager shook hands with her personally and assured her of his intention to raise the subject of credit cards at the next meeting.

'Jesus,' was Mrs Casey's verdict, 'how do I stick living out here in the back of beyond!'

Finally, they went for coffee. Josephine was laden down with plastic bags. She glowed with delight and skipped two or three steps as they came into the café. It was her first time in one and she looked around with interest at the people seated at tables, some with newspapers or magazines, with coffee cups, teapots, cakes, bread, quiches. There were faded old photographs of the town on the wooden walls. Some showed horses walking up the middle of the street. Others showed the little harbour full of old wooden boats with ragged black or brown sails. The walls had a wainscot of reddened pine to about four feet and above that the plasterwork was deliberately roughened to make the place look like a converted stable. A brown wickerwork fan twirled on the ceiling generating a tiny breeze that flattened the steam from their coffees.

'Ah,' said Mrs Casey, 'civilisation. God I hate living out in the sticks. Do you know when I came first you couldn't buy garlic in that shop in the village. Imagine! Life without garlic!'

'Have a sticky bun,' she told Josephine. She brought her back up to the counter and ordered two Danish pastries and a chocolate éclair. She ate one Danish pastry herself. Josephine tasted the coffee carefully. It had what she thought of as a brown flavour. She did not like it but was determined to acquire the taste. Coffee-drinking was a sign of sophistication – only country people drank tea. She imagined herself recounting the experience to Susan, adopting the foreign precision of Ingrid Bergman – 'But it was my first coffee, Susan. It was quite wonderful.' And Susan's smile gleamed at her, glad of the second-hand experience.

Suddenly Mrs Casey sat upright and laughed. She waved at someone behind Josephine's back. Josephine felt something squeezing against the back of her chair. She was aware of a stomach close to the back of her head. Then a man was asking the people at the next table if they needed a spare chair, twisting it around and sitting down.

'How're the ladies?' the man said. He was about the same age as Mrs Casey, dressed in a pinstripe suit with shiny lapels. There were two biros in his breast pocket. Josephine remembered that she had not been allowed to use biros at school at first. Pen and ink, the Master used to say, and the humble pencil – good enough for anyone. And he had found the biro with which that girl had written her name and the word 'bitch' on the toilet wall. And then one day it was all biros. That was in fifth class. Someone even had a single pen with four different colours in it.

'This is our Josephine,' Mrs Casey said, smiling broadly. 'Remember, I mentioned her.'

'The good housekeeper,' the man said. 'Well hello Josephine.' He held out his hand and shook Josephine's. 'I hear you're God's gift to the busy mother.'

Josephine laughed.

'Mr Malone is a family friend,' Mrs Casey said. 'And the family solicitor as well.'

'Counsel to the rich and famous,' Mr Malone said. He looked around and snapped his finger at a waitress who was clearing a nearby table. 'Black coffee, miss,' he said.

'Do we need anything?' Mrs Casey asked Josephine. 'Don't we need flour? And those copies Jean has to get? The ones with the lines on one side and no lines on the other? What do you call it?'

'Nature copies,' Josephine said.

'Exactly. Nature copies. Finish up that bun and run down to the supermarket. Here.' She opened her handbag and took out a five pound note. 'That's enough, is it?'

Josephine said that it was plenty. She left her coffee and half-finished éclair with obvious reluctance and wove her way out between the now crowded tables. The street outside was sullen under a lowering sky. Cars were stopped by a lorry trying to manoeuvre past a narrow point on the street. Their exhausts were acrid and the air had a bluish tinge. She wandered along the street gazing into shop windows and dreaming about her new clothes. She wondered about Mrs Casey's credit card: could you buy anything with it? Could anybody use it? (She remembered Mrs Casey signing her name, but how would the shop assistant know it was the right signature?) How much could you spend?

She went into the supermarket and wandered around the shelves in a daze, finally settling on four or five items that she needed. She had not realised that there was such a variety of things to buy and that each thing came in such a variety of forms. She wandered through the hardware section picking up useful things and putting them down again. She was amazed that there were things in which to dry dishes, little racks and collapsible trays; steel shapes that punched tiny animals out of dough; tins for storing tea and spaghetti; corkscrews that injected air into bottles. She remembered Mrs Casey saying that she couldn't get garlic when she came first, so Josephine bought a long piece of straw rope that had a dozen heads of garlic threaded into it. She bought it from her own money, carefully counting it out and keeping it separate to the change from the five pound note.

Now she understood why Mrs Casey always did the shopping. Each Friday Mrs Casey set out in her car on what she called her 'expedition'. She would come home very late, laden with shopping bags, sometimes smelling of spirits. Josephine loved unpacking the bags, never knowing what would come from them next. Often there were items that she had never seen or heard of before. A tube of paté de foie gras. A jar of pickled onions. A bag of tiny oranges. A frozen duck. 'This is the future,' Mrs Casey often said, pointing at some new food or utensil. 'With the EEC we're going to turn into a modern country. Everything will change.' Josephine had heard her arguing with a friend of the doctor's the year before. It was about the referendum. 'We signed away our birthright in 1973,' she was saying. 'And good riddance to bad rubbish! 1973 will go down as the year we grew up.' But until today Mrs Casey had kept the real secret to herself: the joy of this Aladdin's cave. Josephine wondered if she could arrange to buy the groceries in future, whether Mrs Casey would share with her. If this was what the EEC brought, she was for it too.

When she arrived back at the café Mrs Casey and the solicitor were deep in conversation. The solicitor had both of his elbows on the table and was leaning across it. They had pushed the cups and plates into an untidy jumble in the middle. They started back suddenly when they saw Josephine winding her way through the now almost empty tables. As she put her bags down a waitress asked her if she wanted anything and Josephine shook her head.

'Well Josephine,' the solicitor said. 'Did you get your messages?'

Josephine ignored his question. 'I got you a present Mrs Casey,' she said. 'For all the nice things you bought me.' She took the straw rope threaded with garlic from one of the bags and handed it to Mrs Casey. The words 'You don't have to say you love me,' sang from the imitation teak speaker dangling over their heads. 'Just because you care.'

'Dusty Springfield,' Josephine said. 'Greatest hits.'

Mrs Casey looked at the rope of garlic and then at the solicitor. He made a strange sound, like a suppressed sneeze and looked away. Mrs Casey said, 'Thank you Josephine. That's very kind. How well you knew I liked garlic. And it's so hard to get in the village. We'll be cooking with garlic for a month after this.'

Josephine wasn't sure whether that was a good thing or not. She studied Mrs Casey's face for any sign of a joke and finding it composed and serious she took comfort from it. The solicitor had been taken by a fit of coughing but when he recovered he said that he looked forward to coming out for dinner some night and tasting some of that garlic. Josephine put it back into the plastic bag and smiled contentedly.

'My goodness,' Mrs Casey said suddenly, 'look at the time! Jean will be home before we get back. Come on Josephine. We'd better saddle up.'

'No better woman in the saddle,' the solicitor told Josephine and was immediately doubled up with a fit of coughing again. When he recovered he added that she had an excellent seat as long as she had the reins in her hands.

On the way home Mrs Casey hummed a song and steered wildly, the pitch of the tune rising with each wild swing. When they came to the village crossroads she swung left rather than right. 'We'll go right past the school,' she said. 'We'll meet her along the way.'

She struck the steering wheel with the flat of her hand. 'Giddy up horsey,' she shouted, 'you have the best horsewoman in the county!' She laughed loudly at the thought.

The lone figure of Jean came into sight shortly after they passed the school. She seemed to be equidistant from two small groups of children from her class, obviously ignoring them. She had a brown anorak and an orange knapsack on her back, and was walking carefully along the grassy verge, her eyes on the ground. Even from a distance her shape was discouraging. Mrs Casey fell silent as they coasted ahead of her. When the car came to a stop tilted slightly by the height of the verge, she looked back apprehensively in the mirror. Josephine opened the back door and the child got in, swinging the knapsack off. She did not look up at her mother or Josephine.

'How was school?' Mrs Casey asked as the car pulled out.

'Fine.'

'Much homework?'

'No.'

'Any news at all?'

'No.'

They drove home in silence. The doctor was there before

them, three or four cars parked at the side of the house where he had built on a small surgery. His car was parked at the front. 'His majesty is in residence,' Mrs Casey said. The kitchen radio was blaring when they came in – a girl had disappeared in the Wicklow mountains. The beautiful names: Glen of the Downs; Sally Gap, The Wicklow Way. Josephine pictured the sombre moorland, the trickling water; the occasional blush of heather. Cherry McAllister was the girl's name. An American student. She would be dead, Josephine thought. Her bright American clothes glowing in the brown sludge of a bog-hole.

EIGHT

Josephine was nervous of the babble of voices. She knocked timidly and it was clear after a moment that the teacher had not heard the knock. She rapped again, with her knuckles this time, and the babble diminished. She heard a child say, 'There's someone at the door, Miss.'

'*Oscail an doras*,' said a severe adult voice. The door swung open and an excited child looked out. 'It's a girl, Miss,' she said.

The teacher stood up with a puzzled look. 'What can I do for you?' she said. At the same time she came forwards and signalled to the child to sit down. '*Ciúnas*,' she barked. She came out into the corridor and half-closed the door behind her. Immediately the babble of voices increased.

'I came about Jean Casey,' Josephine said. 'Mrs Casey

couldn't come. They're away on holidays and I'm in charge.'
She paused. 'The doctor has a locum.'

The teacher looked irritated. 'Who might you be?'

'I'm Josephine Strane. I mind Jean. I'm the housekeeper.'
Sometimes Josephine wondered how that had happened. In the
beginning she had been employed to mind the baby and do
light housework. At that time there had been a woman who
came in three times a week. Then the woman's arthritis had
worsened and Josephine took over more of her work. She was
needed and it got to the stage where Mrs Casey could not do
without her. Lately she had begun to teach her to cook. And
Jean was more of a handful too. Although she had never been
perfect. People used to say that: 'Look at her! She's like a little
doll!' That's what you think, Josephine would say to herself. But
she never let on. No point in telling other people your business.
Keep yourself to yourself, Auntie Mary used to say. Mind your
own business.

The teacher stepped back into the room and glared at the
class. 'Do ye want extra homework?' she said. 'Sit down
Thomas. Do you want a slap?' The teacher's skin was perfect,
almost translucent. She had a fine line of cherry exactly marking
her lips and another line of charcoal marking her eyebrows.
When she spoke her eyebrows arched and her lips turned down
in distaste.

'No, Miss' a little boy said.

'I'll send you up to the Master.'

She half-closed the door again. 'Sorry. You were saying?'

'I was saying I'm the housekeeper. I'm in charge while Dr and Mrs Casey are away.'

'I wanted to talk to the parents.'

'They're in Majorca,' Josephine said, as if the teacher could telephone them. The teacher tutted impatiently, then shrugged her shoulders.

'It's about Jean,' she said.

'Was she bold?'

The teacher shook her head. 'The opposite.'

Josephine looked puzzled. 'She's good so?'

'She never puts a foot astray. But that's part of it too. She's too quiet. She never says a word. I get the impression she's frightened of me. And I needn't tell you she has no need to be.'

Josephine Strane, the Master used to say, what will I ever do with you? You're no good to God nor man. And he would sit beside her and guide her through her sums. You're a dunce, he would say, cuffing her lightly on the shoulder and smiling weakly. Isn't it a good job they abolished the Primary Cert or you'd never get out of this place at all? But I'll say one thing for you, you're neatness personified. Now, seven sixes is forty-two, look, write down two and carry four . . . But now she could do them with Jean. She could spell and add and when Jean was older she would be able to multiply and divide. Why couldn't she do them for herself when she was Jean's age? A dunce. Years ago it seemed, those days in the classroom: see how far she had come.

'Well, at least she's good.'

'But there's another problem.'

The teacher pursed her lips and lifted one foot so that the high-heeled shoe hung loose. She leaned the toe of the shoe against her ankle. Her cheeks reddened.

'The thing is, she wet herself last week. The first week back in September she did the same. It happened again yesterday. If I as much as talk to her it happens. And I checked around and I don't think anybody is at her or anything. I can't understand it. And there's another thing now, she always has her homework done perfectly but she's not able to do it in class. That's a mystery now.' She paused.

Josephine said, 'I do the homework with her. I make sure she does it neat and tidy.'

'That's great.'

'I might be helping her a bit too much.'

'I often find that. I often find that mammies and daddies help a bit too much. You might be better off leaving her on her own a bit.' Again the teacher waited.

'I can't do that,' Josephine said. 'She's too messy altogether. She destroys everything. Anyway Mrs Casey says I have to help her.'

'Well well. She's a very polite little girl.'

There had been one girl who knew more than the rest. 'Josey

Strane bitch,' she had written. But Josephine did not care. Show me your company and I'll tell you what you are, Auntie Mary used to say.

'That's good anyway.'

'It is. That's good all right. She's a lovely little thing really. She's a credit to you.'

'I'll try to get her to stop the other business. I noticed it once. I could smell it in her knickers that time. But the other times I didn't. That was in September. She said she couldn't get out to the toilet that time.'

The teacher was horrified. 'Oh no, that's not true at all. Oh no. I'd never do that at all.' Josephine felt a small current of power: the teacher was nervous.

'The little minx,' she said. 'She's a terrible fibber at times.'

'Oh no, she shouldn't have said that at all. I always let them out when they ask.' Josephine sensed that this was a lie.

'Anyway, I'll get her to stop.'

'It's only a matter of self-control,' the teacher said. 'Some of them never learn it. And I might as well tell you some of them do it to get attention. Does she ever wet the bed at night?'

A sly look came over Josephine's face. She shook her head. 'Never,' she said. Mind your own business. That was the name of a plant too.

'You can get a sheet,' the teacher said absently. 'You can even get an electric shock thing that wakes them up.'

'She never wets the bed,' Josephine said. 'I'd notice that straightaway.'

'That's funny,' the teacher said.

'I'll get her to stop,' Josephine said.

'Do.' The teacher stepped back inside the classroom and glared, then stepped back out again. 'There's no need to say you were talking to me.'

Outside in the playground the sunshine was brittle. There was an oily smell that Josephine identified as coming from the chimney of a small growling boiler-house. The infant classes were coming out to play, each class emerging into the light with a stern teacher at its head, one an elderly woman with a tight tweed skirt and twin-set, the other a thin man with a thin mouth and a corduroy jacket with leather elbow-patches. When the last child had come out the two teachers turned their backs on them and began to pace together across the yard, heads leaning towards each other, deep in conversation. Josephine watched the children for a time, their flawless faces, their eager running hither and thither, the furious energy of their collisions and evasions. She saw their skipping games and their jumping games and the chaotic game of football that developed among a group of boys in one corner. She recognised in them something that was absent in herself, and felt a great sucking maw of desolation opening in her. When she moved off under the glare of the teachers who had walked to the end of the yard and swung round to come back, she moved out on to the road and looked longingly at childhood, like a barren woman gazing at someone else's perfect children.

The sun went in as she walked back to the doctor's house and a low cloud settled above the trees. The air was sullen and heated. Roadside furze bushes were glowing yellow filaments and thunder rumbled in the distance before she reached the door. But there was no rain. Instead everything seemed over-charged. The day lost its subtlety.

Josephine waited in the kitchen for the child to come home from school. She watched anxiously for the first sign of rain, ready to run on to the road with the little coat the child had left behind in the morning. She had fried leftover potatoes in a pan with chopped onions. The smell filled the kitchen and drifted out into the hall. Josephine tended the pan with care, using a wooden spatula to lift and turn the potatoes constantly so that they did not stick to the bottom but heated right through. When she was finished they were as white and light as when she started except that they were shot through with the slivers of the cooked onions like translucent finger-parings.

The front door opened and the child came in. She put her school sack down on a chair in the hall. She had an expression-less face, dull greyish skin, lank hair.

Josephine held the frying pan in her left hand and lowered it to show to the child. 'Colcannon,' she said. 'Your favourite.'

'Yummy,' the child said. She climbed up on a kitchen chair and sat looking expectantly at Josephine.

'You did your wee in your pants yesterday again,' Josephine said.

Tears came suddenly to the girl's eyes. She bit her lip and shook her head.

'The teacher said you did.'

'I didn't,' the girl said. Her voice was uncertain, wavering between tears and defiance.

'You did. You did it in front of the whole class,' she said. 'Just like a little baby.'

Now the girl was crying. She was shaking her head. 'No no no,' she said.

'Show me your knickers,' Josephine said. 'Come on. Show them to me.'

The girl stepped down obediently from the chair and lifted her dress.

'Thanks be to God you didn't do it today anyway,' Josephine said.

'I can't help it,' the girl said.

'Do you know what she said. She said I should buy a thing that would give you an electric shock every time you did it. I have half a mind to do it too.'

The girl was trembling.

'Get up to bed this minute,' Josephine said. 'I'm giving this to the dog. You should be ashamed of yourself. You don't deserve to get colcannon. You're a bad bad girl. I'm going to have to tell your mother about you, after all. She'll murder you. Go on. Get up to bed. Say your night prayers for you won't be coming down again tonight.'

Later Josephine heard the child crying. She nodded her head solemnly. 'I'm too easy on you,' she said to herself.

She settled down to watch the early feature film on television. It was an exciting story of a man called Uncle Charlie who tried to kill his niece. Josephine was convinced from the opening scene, which showed Uncle Charlie stretched out on a bed, motionless except for a cigar, that the man was a vampire. She noticed how he lay completely rigid, hands folded across his stomach the way Count Dracula lay in his coffin, how he hid his face from the light when the landlady drew the curtains. His clothes were black and his face expressionless, Middle European looking. She had seen several vampire movies and thought she could recognise one when she saw it. From the moment he worked his way into the heart of his niece's family and began his attempts to kill her, Josephine was on the edge of her seat. She ate her tea in front of the television, wolfing her food in time to the climactic music.

Before the film was over lightning seared the night sky, flashes so brief there was no way of knowing whether they were real or imagined, no matter how much she waited for them. Thunder tumbled afterwards, God rolling a great drum across the roof. Then rain, huge, blank rain, filling the night time, falling straight down without any angle or tilt, streaming in downpipes and spilling out of the weedy gutters. She found the newspaper and looked up that night's programmes for the name of the film. *Shadow of a Doubt*, she read, starring Joseph Cotton and Teresa Wright, dir. Alfred Hitchcock.

When the rain stopped she went up to the child's room. As always she caught her breath at the beauty of it. 'Like something out of one of Mrs Casey's *Homes & Gardens*,' she often said. The room was decorated in a pale, almost translucent pink, with a broad border at about waist height, a pattern of children's toys and funny animals that Mrs Casey brought from London on one of her trips. There was a shiny rocking horse with a blue saddle and gleaming steel stirrups, a row of dolls dressed in expensive clothes including the queen of them all, a beautiful Cindy doll whose clothes could be changed every day for a fortnight. Cindy's clothes were laid out in a tiny but perfect doll's chest of drawers, which was exactly like the mahogany chest that stood at the end of the child's bed. The bed itself was quite ordinary, but the bedhead was plush, quilted satin, a pale pink to match the walls.

She stood at the dark door listening to the uneven breathing and said, 'My poor pet.' She was flooded with pity for the child then. She said it three times. She opened the door wider so that the light from the landing fell on the little head. She could see that the eyes were swollen. She tiptoed in and sat down on the bed. She touched the lank hair and murmured, 'My poor pet.' She stroked the child's forehead. The tiny face was so fragile in repose, trusting and guileless.

Then she became aware of the sweet smell. She looked around her. 'Well God Almighty,' she said. She stood up and caught the blankets beside the child's face. In a sudden violent movement she whipped the blankets up and threw them over the end of the bed. The movement was so swift and supple that the child did not at first wake up. Josephine stared at the dark irregular stain that surrounded the child's waist. She thought of Mrs Casey's reaction, how once she had found the moist sheets and screamed at Josephine. 'What are you doing to my Jean?' Josephine was terrified by the accusation. 'Nothing Mrs Casey! I swear!' she cried. And then Mrs Casey had relented and said she was not to say anything to the doctor, it would be their secret. 'It happens sometimes,' she said. 'Even well-trained children have lapses. This was a little lapse, that's all.'

Suddenly Jean was awake. She sat up and screamed. She put her hands to her face. Josephine struck them down and held them by her sides. 'YOU DID IT AGAIN!' she shouted. 'Look! You wet the bed! Get out you little bitch!' She slapped her across the face twice. 'Get out! Get out!'

When the child scrambled from the bed Josephine tore the sheet off. 'Take that with you!' she hissed. 'You know where to go.'

The child bundled up the sheet and went out. After a moment Josephine heard the bathroom door close. 'Remember,' she shouted, 'that's where you'll sleep every time you wet that bed. Every single time.' She heard the bolt closing on the inside of the bathroom door. She sat down on the edge of the bed and put her face in her hands. 'What am I going to do with her?' she wailed. 'What am I going to do at all?'

NINE

First the air was full, tempting, slightly charged: then there was mist, effusive, complete. The space between the window and the trees no longer existed. Josephine stared out and wondered where it all came from and how had she missed its arrival. Upstairs Jean was wailing, a long high ululation, followed by a near-silence that she knew was really the low moaning that did not travel beyond the door or the bedroom walls. Mrs Casey was there still. Sometimes she could hear her voice, more throbbing than soothing. Soon she would call again: a change of sheets; more ice; empty the basin. The demands were increasingly desperate, the voice closer to histrionic.

Josephine heard the sound of a racing engine somewhat muffled by the drizzle and saw the doctor's car swing off the road suddenly, racing up the drive, headlights on full, wipers going full tilt. It came to a halt in a grinding of pebbles at the front door and the doctor jumped out. He opened the back door and took out his bag. Josephine held the front door for him but he pushed past her.

'I got the message at Donovan's,' he said. 'Fever. Pain in the neck. Is that it?' He was already halfway up the stairs.

'Vomiting,' Josephine said.

She saw him disappear around the bend in the stairs and heard Jean's bedroom door open and close. 'Don't turn on the light!' she shouted after him. 'It hurts her eyes.'

Months pass, she thought, and nothing happens. Days when the sizzle of the fat in the oven or the burbling of water in a saucepan are the only sounds. The doctor comes and goes bringing life or death to other people's children. How long was it since the teacher had told her that it was all a matter of self-control? Months? Six months? And while the doctor's back was turned and Mrs Casey was away something had got in and poisoned Baby Jean. There was no controlling this thing. It boiled up through her skin in red blotches. She spewed yellow bile and spoiled everything.

After five minutes he came down and she heard him talking to the hospital. He went back upstairs then only to come down five minutes later. He called the hospital again and she heard him tell them to cancel the ambulance. He came into the kitchen, his face flushed with fear. He was a tall heavy-set man, hair greying in flashes along the side of his head. There was something of the build of a rugby-player in him, the slope shoulders, the thick neck. His face was set into a permanent expression of warmth, the necessary creases and lines etched there by ten thousand house-calls.

'Get extra blankets and a bag of ice. A plastic bag,' he said. 'And a plastic bucket.'

There was a yellow sand-bucket in the shelf below the sink. Last summer they had all gone to Wexford for a long weekend and Mrs Casey had bought a set of sand-tools for Jean, a rake with a wooden handle and plastic head, three moulds of animals that left strange misshapen marks in the wet sand, a shovel and the bucket. They had spent each day sitting on Curracloe beach watching the sun shimmering on the water and the little drifting fishing boats with their single tan-coloured steadying sail working the shallows for shellfish. At night Josephine had stayed with Jean while the doctor and his wife went out, usually to a restaurant or to the local pub. They would come home late and morose and sleep late in the morning. The sand-bucket had not been used since and Josephine had taken to keeping things in it, the Brillo pads, a scouring brush, the plunger for the kitchen sink. She did not know what the doctor wanted the bucket for.

Soon the two of them came down the stairs. He was carrying Jean wrapped in blankets, a bundle of sticks, a bag of bones. She moaned with every step. 'No time to waste,' he said. 'We'll take her in the car.'

They drove at high speed along the main road, the doctor blaring the horn at every turn. Mrs Casey sat in the back cradling Jean's head on her lap. Jean did not vomit again though there was some empty retching, the gulping sound echoing hollow in the bright yellow sand-bucket.

They were halfway to town when the doctor said, 'You weren't at your mother's?'

Mrs Casey said, 'For God's sake, this is no time Peter.'

'Josephine knew.'

Josephine stared at the flickering gates and ditches.

'She knew where to ring.' His knuckles were white around the brown leather of the steering wheel.

'When did this start?' To Josephine. She tried to think. Last night certainly, Jean had soiled the bed, a spume of yellow vomit on the edge of the blanket and rolled into the sheet. She was still half-asleep when Josephine came in, only partially aware that something unusual had happened. Josephine slapped her and sent her to the bathroom with the sheet, but quickly realised that there would be no hiding it. She stripped the blankets and got new ones and remade the bed. When she went to the bathroom she found Jean asleep on the floor, her head canted out at an unusual angle as though stretching away from the rest of her body. She eased the sheet from her grasp and carried her back to bed. She sat by her side for a time, combing the hair off her forehead with the flat of her palm and wondering what Mrs Casey would say to the blankets and the dirty sheet. Dirt brings disease, she had said. Josephine wondered if Jean had the osteomyelitis now. Would she finish up with a limp in her hip? Where did the dirt come from? Mrs Casey's father had been a doctor and he brought the disease home.

Jean was listless, and breathing rapidly, and under her chin, in the soft white skin of her neck, there were two jagged red blisters, like small bites.

'Do you mean to tell me,' Dr Casey hissed when she told him, 'that that child was sick last night and you never told anyone?'

Jean was moaning and feverish by midnight and Josephine was possessed by a fierce joy. Mrs Casey was away, visiting her mother, and Dr Casey was at a doctors' dinner-dance in town. She had Jean all to herself, complete control over the little body. The doctor would not be home until late and would be gone on his rounds by nine o'clock in the morning. That left a gap of no more than a few wakeful hours when the house would be in the possession of someone else. She was overcome by a tumult of emotions. She lay down beside little Jean and stroked her head and murmured to her. She knew now that she could have the sheets and blankets cleaned and possibly even dried before Mrs Casey came home. She had seen such sicknesses before, Jean being peculiarly susceptible to whatever gastro-enteritis was going through her school. By the time the doctor returned for his afternoon surgery tomorrow, she, Josephine, would have dealt with the problem. No one would ever know. 'My poor pet,' she whispered over and over again, sweeping the sweat-soaked hair off the child's forehead. She thought of Susan lying on her own bed, her eyes shut, her long lashes down. She wished Jean could be as still and calm as Susan, lying without pain in a perfect sleep. Susan needed her completely. She could not wake unless Josephine held her. And now, for a short time, this child was orphaned too, relying for everything on Josephine Strane.

'You're the bloody doctor anyway!' Mrs Casey said. 'Don't be blaming it on Josephine!'

'How could I do anything when I didn't know! Jesus Christ woman!'

'Don't talk to me like that!'

'How should I talk so? What? Like I was talking to, to Malone's whoor?'

Mrs Casey made a strange sound, a strangled yelp. Out of the corner of her eye Josephine saw that she was on the point of hitting the back of the doctor's head. Then the car passed over a pothole and Jean screamed and Mrs Casey bent her head and stroked the child's face.

'Oh God!' the doctor said. 'This bloody traffic.' Ahead of them an English tour bus proclaimed a firm from Cornwall as the providers of comfort and every convenience. Even from behind the passengers looked English, familiar and yet foreign, more like Coronation Street than anything Irish. The bus edged along the narrow road with studied English caution, the wheels extending downwards into the potholes like feet, the carriage of the bus never varying in its evenness. There was a scarf on the back of a headrest that said Everton.

The doctor slammed his hand on the side panel of the door and said, 'Every second counts. I gave her a shot of penicillin just in case, but I'm fairly sure.'

'Pull out,' Mrs Casey said. 'You're a doctor. Pull out around the traffic.' But he did not pull out.

'There's a guard up ahead at the junction,' he said. 'That's what has it the way it is.'

'For Jesus's sake tell him it's an emergency,' she said. But the traffic cleared suddenly once they passed the guard. The Cornish bus swung left and then the road ahead was clear and Dr Casey said, 'Thanks be to Christ!' Jean moaned as the car accelerated and Mrs Casey said, 'Hurry.'

'The last thing we want is a tip,' the doctor said. 'The last thing we want is for me to hit something.'

At the emergency door of the hospital they were waiting with a stretcher, two men in white coats and three nurses. Jean screamed uncontrollably when they moved her. Her head barely moved. Her skin was paper dry. When the stretcher rolled in under the fluorescent striplights she put her left hand over her eyes.

Mrs Casey and Josephine sat in a kind of grey-green limbo, on chairs with imitation-plastic leather that made their clothes wet from perspiration. Mrs Casey moaned and wept as though she were sick herself. She kept asking Josephine what she should do. Nurses and doctors passed them by and the chairs and benches filled and emptied, mostly walking wounded: a man with a bleeding eye; a man with broken leg; a woman with steam-scalded hands; a child who had swallowed something; someone who had been in a motorbike accident and had minor cuts and abrasions, mostly on the face; a woman with a black eye and a split lip who kept holding her stomach and making vomiting sounds; a child who had been bitten on the lip by a dog; an elderly woman who had collapsed on the street. At the nursing station they had a radio turned down low and Josephine counted off the time by the number of songs she heard, allowing on average three minutes per song and a half minute in between. Once they played Don Maclean's 'American Pie' and she knew it was eight minutes' long, more or less. She searched in her memory for the exact time, having heard a disc jockey say it some months before, but the memory would not come. She listened to the words and found them inexpressibly sad, full of the tragedy of the moment, the sick child, the wounded and unwell. Bye bye Miss American Pie, she repeated silently when the song was over. Them good old boys were drinkin whiskey and rye and singing this'll be the day that I die.

After an hour the doctor came out, ashen and trembling. 'Maurice Curtin confirmed it,' he said. Mrs Casey began to cry loudly. The doctor looked away, watching the swing doors open and close, following the bustling movements of a nurse carrying a tray of instruments. 'Yes,' he said absently. 'It looks bad enough.'

'What is it Doctor?'

'It's all over the place,' he said. 'Three schools that I know about. Curtin says he has five cases on his hands.'

'Please Doctor?' Josephine said.

He looked at her as if surprised that she was still there. 'Meningitis.'

'Oh Jesus! It's that bad so? said Mrs Casey.'

He nodded. 'Meningococcal meningitis. And there's septicaemia,' he said. 'That's the weals she has.'

'Is it bad?' Josephine was trembling uncontrollably, a visible sovereign palsy that grappled her entire body. 'Is it like osteomyelitis?'

Mrs Casey turned on her and pushed her so sharply that she fell off the chair, sitting down hard on the tiles, one elbow braced on the next chair. 'You dirty bitch,' she shouted. 'Why didn't you tell us?'

Josephine stood up and backed away but Mrs Casey rose too and followed her, backing her against a steel locker. Dr Casey caught her forearm and pulled her back. 'Leave her alone Grace. She thought it was a bug. You couldn't expect her to know.'

'She's always hiding things,' Mrs Casey said. 'She thinks I don't know.'

'What are you talking about?'

'She has all my *Woman's Owns* up in her room. Under the bed. I found them. And *Vogue*.'

'For Christ's sake who cares!' The doctor pulled her back and stood between them, his hands on his wife's shoulders. 'Who cares about the bloody books.'

'The teacher up at the school, she told me things too. That bitch was up there when I was away.'

'She has to go up sometimes.'

'Spying on me! Listening to my phone calls!'

'If you were suspicious of her why didn't you say so? Why Grace? She's only a child.'

Mrs Casey suddenly looked wary. She straightened and shook the doctor's hands off. 'I know about you,' she said to Josephine. 'You needn't think you're fooling me.'

An elderly man in a white coat came into the waiting room and paused at the threshold. He looked from Mrs Casey to her husband. He coughed gently. He took Dr Casey aside and they spoke quietly for a moment, then he went back through the swing doors.

'They're doing the best they can, Grace,' Dr Casey said. 'We're only in the way. They're giving her a penicillin drip now. That'll hit it on the head. We're only in the way here. We should go home and leave it to the professionals.'

'I'm not leaving my child, if that's what you're thinking. You go home to your bed. I'm staying here.'

'You won't be able to see her.'

'I'm not leaving.'

Dr Casey cursed under his breath and gestured to Josephine. Together they moved towards the exit but at the door he whirled round and stood, red-faced, staring at her, struggling to say what was on his mind or control it.

'Go on,' she said contemptuously. 'A doctor needs a good night's rest.'

'Jesus Christ,' he said. 'You were quick enough to leave her alone when that cunt Malone was sniffing around – sniffing around you like a bitch in heat.'

'Who told you where to ring?' Mrs Casey hissed at Josephine. She advanced two paces. 'Who told you where I was, you dirty little spy?' Josephine turned and burst through the swing doors. Two nurses standing at the corner of the next corridor stared at her in surprise. She ran until she saw the big main doors of the hospital in front of her and she could smell the cool sour smell of wet earth. Then she slowed to a walk. Shortly she heard the clatter of the doctor's leather-soled shoes on the tiles behind her. The footsteps seemed to her to be unhurried. Yes, she thought, doctors never hurry. They have to keep calm.

TEN

Once the phone rang and when she picked it up she knew the voice was that of the priest. She hadn't seen him or her mother since a week after Auntie Mary's funeral. 'Who's this I'm speaking to now?' he said, and she said it was the housekeeper, Josephine Strane. 'The very one I want to talk to,' the voice said. 'I'll get the doctor for you,' Josephine said. 'He's finished surgery. I seen the last car going out ten minutes ago,' 'No no,' the voice said. 'It's yourself I'm after.'

'All right so Father,' Josephine said.

'I have a bit of bad news. A bit of bad news. Not too bad mind. It's about your mother. She had a bit of a turn. She's in the County Home.'

Josephine practised calm. As the priest spoke she was deliberately controlling her breathing, in out in out. She made an effort to think about something nice but her thoughts turned to Jean in the hospital.

'So that's it. A bit of a turn. I was in to her myself last night. I promised her, I promised her I'd let you know.'

'Thanks very much Father. Goodbye.'

The voice in the phone squawked. 'Hold on hold on now.'

'What?'

'Are you coming home? Are you coming back to see her?'

'No.'

'Your own mother!'

'Dr Casey needs me at the minute. My little girl is in hospital recovering from meningitis. The bad kind. I couldn't leave now.'

There was a short pause. Then a quieter voice came back. 'I heard about the poor thing. How is she at all?'

'She's over the worst of it now. She's mending. She'll be perfect when she comes out.'

'I see. And Mrs Casey? How is she taking it?'

Josephine smiled at the coy curiosity of the priest. Everyone knew that Mrs Casey had moved out. There had been a kind of balance, she understood, tipped for ever by Jean's collapse. Josephine knew now that Mrs Casey had become frightened of her, frightened of what she might know. That was why she had been able to keep Jean for herself. And Mrs Casey had let her see the solicitor; that was her big mistake. She was a bad mother and then Josephine had taken her place. But when Josephine phoned the solicitor's house the balance had tipped and Mrs Casey saw that she couldn't stay. Not when everyone knew. She gave Josephine her baby and the doctor. She gave her the house.

'Will I get the doctor for you?' she said. 'I hear him in the kitchen.'

Afterwards Dr Casey said that Josephine must go home. He would manage fine without her for a few days and her mother needed her. She should take a week's holidays and have a bit of a break. Father Jim would collect her himself the following day. That was the arrangement they made over the phone. He spoke kindly but firmly. So Josephine packed a small bag and Father Jim arrived punctually at eleven o'clock. The doctor was in surgery but he came out for a minute to chat to the priest. Then the doctor went back inside and they drove off in the priest's Ford Escort.

It was a bright morning after a rainy night, fields full of brittle light, the distant mountains pencilled against the skyline with childish clumsiness. The priest whistled a tuneless song through a gap in his front teeth, and drove with nerve-wracking prudence, blowing his horn as he nosed through sharp bends and indicating his intention of overtaking long before moving out. An obscure fear had settled on Josephine and she sat jammed in the corner of the passenger seat huddled into the bag on her lap.

'So,' the priest said, 'poor little Jean hah?'

'Yes Father.'

'Dr Casey says there was no mental effect anyhow. That's good anyway.'

'Yes Father.'

'Still and all. He says the marks, the purple marks, they'll fade a bit.'

Susan's lovely face. Pale blue eyes under the elegant lashes. A hint of rouge on the cheek. Full sweet lips. At night sometimes she washed her hair, wetting it under the tap and combing the drops out. And she took the clothes off: the waisted dress of faded sateen draped with organdie, a neck of lace and lace at the wrists; the tiny slip; the long legged cotton knickers nipped at the knee with elastic. Susan lying in a bath of warm water, blue eyes gazing up or closed in joy. There were no blemishes. No marks.

'Still, it's a terrible thing for a woman. Did you ever hear the expression a woman's face is her fortune? That's an old saying. Still, there's plastic surgery of course. Plastic surgery is brilliant nowadays. There was a fellow arrested in Germany there one time, I was reading it in the *Reader's Digest*, and wasn't he a completely different man. Plastic surgery. He got some crooked doctor to make up a completely new face for him. To evade capture.'

Between two low hills Josephine caught a quick glimpse of the sea, distant and faded, a brushstroke of blue between two blobs of burnt umber. A tractor climbed one of them with painful slowness, a sparkling of seagulls in its trail, yellow-green stubble slowly turning into clay.

'Seemingly they knew he was a murderer or whatever because the face was completely dead. No outside emotions at all. That was what Shakespeare said. There is no art to find the mind's construction in the face. You never went to secondary of course. You missed Shakespeare.' He shook his head as though a great tragedy had befallen her.

'To evade capture,' the priest said again. 'Tragic altogether about the little girl. Were you fond of her?'

'She's still alive.'

'I know that I know that. Mrs Casey, I suppose she's staying with friends. To be near the hospital.'

Josephine looked at him and recognised the crafty look as the same that came over her mother's face when she wanted Josephine out of the house for some reason, or when she had got hold of a bottle of some kind and had hidden it. 'She moved in with Malone the solicitor,' she said brutally. 'Malone & Malone, 18 Cross Street, Commissioner for Oaths. She left.'

'Dear me dear me,' the priest said. 'That's shocking. Poor Dr Casey.' But she noticed that he looked satisfied, like a child who had completed a particularly difficult manoeuvre and found sweets in the process.

'That's shocking of course. Immoral. I don't know what the world is coming to at all Josephine. There I was thinking you'd be safe in that house, safe in that house altogether. Tis the way things are going from bad to worse child. That's what it is.'

The priest's bleating did not disturb Josephine. She watched the sea growing in its presence outside the windows, patches of blue caught between hills becoming the flash of waves behind trees and finally the broad sweep of the bay and the sea-wall. There were traces of weed along its top and she remembered seeing a report of a storm on the television recently. The tide was on the ebb and the mud was emerging from under it along the village front, the lower blackened stones of the pier ragged with bladder-wrack.

'What did you have for your breakfast?' the priest said suddenly, as they were passing the pier. 'Don't tell me. Don't tell me now. Was it rashers and sausages?' Josephine said it was. The priest looked very pleased. 'I was right.' He began the tuneless whistling again, watching Josephine slyly from the corner of his eye. After a time he stopped whistling and looked directly at her.

'Well? Are you going to ask me how I know?'

'How do you know Father?'

He laughed. 'I can smell it. I have it down to a fine art. I can always tell what someone had to eat last.' He laughed again. 'What do you think of that?'

'Amazing,' Josephine said.

'Isn't it though?' the priest said.

He dropped her at the door of the County Home and said she knew where to find him if she was stuck for a lift. The implication was that he would not welcome having to drive her all the way back again. He waved gaily to her as he drove away.

The County Home smelled of Jeyes Fluid and urine, old men's clothes and wax polish. A nun walked her to the ward, chatting about the weather. She pointed to an angular bundle in a bed near a window and said, 'It was a stroke. It wasn't the first one either. But she's taking it very well, God bless her.'

Josephine brought a chair from an open space in front of a television set and placed it beside her mother's bed. Her mother was asleep, half-propped by pillows, but canted over to her right, a wax figure melted down one side. Her newly cropped hair that stood up like a series of unravelling wicks emphasised the wax-candle appearance. She made sounds in her sleep, low guttural ejaculations that could have been curses or prayers, and her left hand plucked at the sheets spasmodically.

After a time Josephine turned the chair a little more and watched the television. It was a children's programme, all slant-faced cartoon heroes who spoke and fought in abrupt rhythms and whose world was full of grey and brown. Gradually Josephine became aware that her mother was watching her. She turned and saw that although the old woman had not shifted her place in the bed, her eyes were open and she was staring at her daughter.

'Hi Mammy,' Josephine said. Her mother blinked one eye. The other, her right, looked lazy, the lid drooping like a loose shirt-tail. Josephine noticed that the right-hand side of her mother's face looked loose, slightly folded, a sac of skin rolled between her jaw and the collar of her dressing-gown. 'Are you able to talk?'

'Wwhere wwere you?' her mother asked. Josephine explained that she didn't know about her mother's turn until Father Jim rang last night, that she came down this morning.

'I tol you – ome – fore dark,' her mother said. The words were slurred, indistinct, a sibilant mischief lurking in the slack side of the mouth.

'But Mammy,' Josephine said, 'I'm working with years past.'

Her mother half-smiled. 'Mary – here earlier. Bitch.'

Josephine shook her head. 'Auntie Mary is dead,' she said.

Her mother became agitated. She made an effort to raise herself on to the pillows but seemed to have no strength in the arm she was lying on. Her eyes darted from side to side as though searching for someone.

'Wan gohome,' she said. 'Own bed.'

'Sure of course,' Josephine said. Her eyes wandered to the cartoon again.

Her mother's left hand slapped the counterpane. It was a small sound but it recalled Josephine from the television.

'I – scream,' the old woman demanded. She slapped her hand again. A lazy tongue slipped out and licked one side of her mouth. 'Cold.'

'You had a stroke,' Josephine said calmly. 'You'll finish your days in here. You might as well get used to it. You're lucky they'll keep you. I seen where they put people who see dead people. The mad house, you wouldn't like that?' Her mother's eyes looked small and unsynchronised. She stared at Josephine for a moment, then resumed her searching of the ward. 'I have my own life to lead,' Josephine said. 'I have a sick little girl to mind and I have to look after Dr Casey. I'm the only one left now. Herself ran away with a solicitor. I'm in charge of everything.'

'Die – own bed,' her mother said.

'You'll die here in this bed,' Josephine said. 'Anyway you know well your own bed is filthy, the same as always. I wouldn't let a dog sleep in it. You'll stay here where the nuns look after you. You were never so well off.' She looked around her with a satisfied smile on her face. She saw the orderly rows of beds, the neatly cornered counterpanes, the polished tiles of the floor. The walls reflected green on her face, a deathly pallor. Her mother absorbed none of it, her pale grey skin unchanging in the light. Her eyes gazed aslant imparting a furtive and at the same time baleful appearance to her face. Her right leg and hand flickered in unison. 'I'm well out of it, I can tell you,' Josephine said. 'You led me a dog's life. All the things you did to me, the things I see you do. You were always drinking. I hate drink. Dr and Mrs Casey never drink too much. If they did I'd walk out first thing in the morning. I never see them drunk the way I had to look at you. You were never much of a mother.'

Josephine began to tell her mother of her life as a minder of children and housekeeper to the doctor's family. She emphasised, for her mother's benefit, the difference between the house of her childhood and this new world. She spoke about Dr Casey's insistence on cleanliness, his obsession with germs and the places they grew; the standards the Caseys insisted on such as envelope corners on all the beds; the kinds of food she had learned to cook. She spoke of everything as if it were a kind of school she had been attending, a careful, thorough finishing school.

'I'm beginning to feel as if I'm ready for the world now. And I have a bit of money put by as well,' she said finally. 'It started with the money Auntie Mary left me.' Soothed almost to sleep by Josephine's litany of cleanliness, her mother became suddenly alert. She made an attempt to push herself upright in the bed but the effort dissolved to the right. Her agitation produced only a half-shrugging motion and an increase in the hand-leg rhythm. Josephine watched her for a moment and then stood up.

'I bet you never knew,' she said. 'Auntie Mary was good to me. She showed me the difference between good and bad. She left me five thousand pounds.' Her mother stared now, her left eye enlarged, her right half closed. Her fist had cramped but the index finger remained extended, almost as though she were pointing at something. Josephine laughed. She regretted that she had not said ten. 'Five thousand pounds and you never saw a penny of it. I invested it.' She thought of Dr Casey's investments. He would read share quotations aloud from the newspaper sometimes, remarking that such and such had gone up or down, or that they were paying dividends, or that property was going through the roof. Mrs Casey never seemed to be interested. 'Stocks and shares and property,' she said. 'Property is up again. You can't go wrong with property.' Her mother's agitated finger, the mottled palm slapping the bed.

'I'm going now,' she said. 'I probably won't see you again.' She bent down and whispered into her face. 'Goodbye Mammy.' She felt a wave of pleasure at the words. Goodbye, goodbye, she repeated. 'Parting is such sweet sorrow,' a letter had said. 'How can I say goodbye to my husband?' And what was the answer? You must treasure every moment. As she left she heard the slow-motion snoring, the laboured breathing, the sighs and rustling of elderly people in bed, and over it all she heard the beating of her mother's hands and legs, the staccato of anger; she heard it and walked on, smiling.

ELEVEN

Her mother's house was as if she had never left it, the blinds awry, the furniture thrown into each room without any regard for order. Items of clothing slung on chairs had an expectant look like wraiths waiting patiently for an old friend to pass over. There was a disgusting grime on everything, a lichen-thick film composed of dust and precipitated cooking-fat and cigarette smoke, that gave everything she touched a tacky waxy feel. A loaf of bread on the table had grown a dense livid-blue mould that bristled with silky hairs. The mould had spread along the table surface, finding sustenance in stains and crumbs so that the whole thing seemed to be carpeted in a rich blue texture. Milk in a bottle had separated into a dirty grey-green water and a glutinous white rind. There were rat and mouse droppings everywhere and when she lifted the loaf of bread she found that a cave had been hollowed out of one side.

A magazine was spread on the table and the mould had worked over the edges. 'Tummy Ache?' the article queried. 'Stress could be the answer.' Josephine paused long enough to read the first three paragraphs, lingering lovingly on words like ulcerative colitis and non steroidal anti-inflammatories. A notice in a box in one corner said: Dr Hollis welcomes your questions but due to pressure of work is unable to reply individually. Please do not send an sae. Josephine wondered what an sae was. Then she tore off the polluted edges and threw the magazine on to a chair where she intended putting things to take away.

It didn't take long to find the bottles. Two were standing on a table beside her mother's favourite armchair, hidden by a large empty flower vase. One had an inch of the transparent liquor. The other was almost full. The other two bottles were carefully stowed in different drawers in different rooms, both half-empty. Josephine poured their contents down the sink, the sweet smell filling the kitchen. She brought the four empties out to the backyard and studied the glittering graveyard of gin bottles that her mother had accumulated in the last few years. She could think of no way to get rid of them. She counted eighty-one.

In the end she filled as many pillow cases and plastic bags as she could find and one by one she took them down the road to a quiet place where a stream ran through boggy ground behind a high ditch. It took her over an hour and her hands were sore and her shoulders weary of the effort. With each load she climbed up on to the ditch and, checking first that there was no one around to see, tossed the clanking bags as far as she could into the bog. She laughed when she thought what someone would make of the dump in future years, dozens of empty gin bottles wrapped in Dunnes' Stores bags and pillowcases! She wondered if the bottles would sink below the surface not to be discovered for a thousand years, like the barrel of ancient butter she had read about recently. But she was sure they would be discovered in time because she knew that nothing could be hidden for ever. Not by people. Only death could do that, she knew: bury a secret beyond the reach of the curious.

She cleaned the house as best she could, considering that her mother had only half a bottle of Parazone and no washing-up liquid, polish or scouring cream. She tore a sheet to make dishcloths. When the house was smelling of disinfectant and the surfaces were clean to her satisfaction she arranged the miserable furniture to approximate the order of Dr Casey's house. She pursed her lips in frustration that nothing would quite go into its proper place or be its proper size or shape, but in the end she was placated. Now she knew what she had to do. Putting order on the house gave her a pleasant feeling, as though she had the power to change the past. She knew she would have to go back to the hospital to tidy up one last detail and then she could walk away for ever.

It was now the quiet hour in the afternoon when most of the patients, sated by soup, minced chicken and ice-cream, settled into the profound sleep that was denied to them at night. The ward was sibilant with it, the bodies thrown back against the pillows, translucent eyelids closed, toothless mouths open. They made awkward structures under the blankets, which reminded Josephine of a bag of turkey bones she threw out at Christmas.

Her mother was asleep, still in that posture that suggested one side of her body was shorter than the other. But most of the pillows had been taken away and she now rested on a shallow slope. Afternoon sunlight caused an eerie glow, reflected off the green wall paint, that made her look already dead and partially decayed, like a corpse recovered from prolonged immersion. The aluminium frames that circled each bed had pale blue plastic curtains patterned with stylised palm trees. It seemed to Josephine that she was visiting an aquarium such as she had seen on television. The impression was so intense that she expected to see exotic fish circling outside the window and occasional sly-mouthed rays or sharks nosing the glass.

The idea of stifling her mother did not come to her immediately. She sat for a long time looking at her fingers and nagging a hangnail. Then she studied the patient in the next bed, a dapper-looking elderly woman with a faint hint of blue in her hair, accentuated by the weird light, her head thrown back, her mouth open and appearing to project a soft snoring sound at the ceiling. She poured a glass of water from her mother's jug and drank it all. Finally she sighed and stood up. She took the bundle of *Woman's Weeklys* that she had brought with her from her mother's house out of the Dunnes' Stores plastic bag and placed them flat on the floor. She took a pillow from a stack that stood on an empty bed, shaking her head sadly at the fact that it had no pillow-slip. She placed the plastic bag over her mother's mouth and nose and then the pillow on her face, and then she put her left hand down hard on the place where the open mouth had been. *Whatever Happened to Baby Jane?* she thought, as she bore down on it. Bette Davis and Joan Crawford. Her mother did not utter a sound. The only sign that she was in distress was the beating of hand and leg, a rapid-fire salvo that lasted little more than a minute. While her mother shook Josephine remained steadfast, watching the oscillations of a lustrous nut-brown feather that had worked out of the coarse weave of the pillow. It seemed to her that the feather was shivering in the ghost of her mother's breathing.

The lack of a struggle consoled Josephine and she smiled a sad small smile to herself as she returned the pillow to its stack. She thought her mother had slipped away quietly, perhaps with less pain and distress than a natural death would have brought. She consoled herself that what she had done was an act of mercy. And she thought of death the secret-keeper and the yellow earth that was her grandmother and of how her aunt's coffin had gone down at last, effortlessly taking its appointed place in the soil.

When she was finished she put the *Woman's Weeklys* back into the plastic bag, wiping away the snot and spittle on the trailing edge of her mother's sheet. She took her mother's hands from inside the sheet, grumbling at the awkwardness of manipulating unco-operative bones, and folded them across her chest. The hands would not lie straight because of the waxwork melting of her mother's body, drifting sideways on to the counterpane each time. Josephine looked around but could see nothing that would hold them in place. 'A bit of Sellotape,' she murmured. But Sellotape would give the game away. In the end she let them fall together, folded slightly into each other, almost like someone relaxed in prayer. She stepped back and studied the effect and was satisfied. On her way out she took a newspaper from a bedside locker and then went to the nursing station further down the corridor.

'I got a bit of a fright,' she told the drowsy nurse. 'When I went in my mother was dead.'

The nurse was on her feet and moving before Josephine could finish her story. 'At least I think she was anyway,' she shouted. The nurse did not turn round. Josephine watched her padding hastily towards the ward, clicking the top of a biro agitatedly, and noted that her rump bulged in the white uniform, twin bulges at the side of each thigh and twin buttocks outlined and shaded by the sub-layer of grey-black that must have been the nurse's underpants, two more bulges just behind the armpits. Her tennis shoes were white but there was mud on the sole.

On the bus she read the newspaper from cover to cover. Under the heading of Personal in the advertising pages she found an advertisement that interested her.

Nanny needed by American couple coming to live and work in Ireland. One child dearly loved. References required. Ph. 352367 ext. 234

The bus rattled along, shaking the six or seven elderly passengers clutching their shopping bags and plastic macs. They smiled benignly at her and she smiled back. Once a foreign-looking young man with a backpack got on and the instant firming of the air was palpable – a stiffening of shoulders, eyes turned to the newsreel of the passing road, a short silence followed by hurried artificial conversation. When he got off at a village post office the conversation revived again, glances followed his angular back as he walked along the street the bus was following, keeping pace for a time in order to provide them with subject matter for their hostility.

Josephine studied the advertisement and daydreamed about the word 'nanny'. She thought of herself in a white uniform, caring for a perfect child with beautiful teeth who spoke exactly like John F. Kennedy. She imagined a house such as she had seen on television in manicured American suburbs that had no hedges, huge open rooms, a modern kitchen. The father would work in a book-lined study complete with leather couch and chairs. She had seen exactly the right kind of study in *The Virginian.* Judge Garth sat in it, dispensing justice and wisdom to his ranch-hands and neighbours, a steady kindly man. There were button-back chairs and books with leather covers and gold lettering on the spine and sunlight beyond the windows. The doors would slide open and vanish, as if by magic, into apertures in the walls. She imagined the child growing up and blossoming under her care.

Later she told Dr Casey of her intention of applying for the job. He shrugged his shoulders and said that he couldn't blame her. He looked miserable, unable to meet her gaze. He went out and came back with a large glass of whiskey and topped the glass up with water from the tap. He drank a third of the glass in one gulp and made a grimace and shivered slightly. Then he sipped it and said, 'With poor Jean and all, and just myself in the house, I couldn't ask you to stay. I know very well what the biddies around here will be saying.'

'Oh no, Dr Casey,' Josephine said. 'No one would ever say anything against you. But I have to go on with my career.' She heard the radio playing 'Money Can't Buy You Love'. The Beatles, she thought, the name registering as a tiny voice at the same time as she heard Dr Casey say, 'Of course you do, of course you do. You have to think of yourself.' The glass was now half-empty and he topped it up with more tap water. 'You needn't fear for a reference. I'll write one for you and welcome. Welcome.'

'Oh thanks very much Doctor. That's a load off my mind. I was worried that you might blame me for Jean being sick. Because I was in charge.'

He shook his head. 'It could have happened to anyone. Never mind what Grace says. She's only saying those things because she feels guilty about the whole thing. Not being here when it happened and . . . and everything.'

Josephine said nothing. She did not know what Mrs Casey had been saying about her.

He waved his glass at her. 'You're young still,' he said. 'You have your whole life in front of you.' Josephine thought that Dr Casey had not much of his life left, an old man, ageing more quickly now that his wife was gone with the solicitor. She thought she detected the mark of death on him, the ineffable folding of the spirit that led to collapse. She had seen it in her aunt's dead face, and in the wet face of her mother. She thought it was sad.

Suddenly, the doctor's shoulders began to shudder and his lips turned down in a comical sulk, pulling down his cheeks and eyes and causing his chin to jut out so that he looked like a cartoon exaggeration of himself, a kind of Neanderthal in a shirt and tie. Josephine looked at him for a moment, slightly repulsed by the ugliness of his grief, by his willingness to expose his hurt to her. She saw him chew his lips trying to control his emotion and when, for a brief moment, his control failed, she saw a glob of spittle break free and drop on to his shirt.

'Oh Doctor,' Josephine said, 'she'll come running back soon enough. Just you wait and see.'

TWELVE

'Your reference is excellent,' Robert Fraser said. He flashed an abbreviated smile at her, a gleam of teeth and then his face recomposed itself. 'Dr Casey. A medical doctor?'

'Yes.'

'From? Where exactly is this place?'

'It's about thirty miles away.'

'He says here that you saved his daughter's life. How did that happen?'

'It wasn't like that at all. She was very sick and I noticed there was something wrong. That's all it was.'

'What was it?'

'It was meningitis.'

A sharp intake of breath. 'I guess that's sick enough. And you had it spotted?' Josephine lowered her head and said nothing. 'I guess you're alert to that kind of thing. That's good.'

'It's common enough,' she said. 'I read about it in *Good Housekeeping*. We're all carrying it around in our nose. But some people get it as a disease and nobody knows why.'

'But it's really dangerous? People die from it?'

'One in ten,' Josephine said. Her left foot began a small jig on the floor. She was thinking, Now that I've found you I can let you go. The Foundations, 1967. The insistent rhythm drew Robert Fraser's eyes.

'Tell me about your family Miss Strane.'

Josephine cleared her throat and looked straight at him. 'I come from a poor family Mr Fraser. Don't think I come from money. My father died when I was only four and my mother worked hard to bring us up right. I was the oldest one of us and I had to do my bit. You could say I was minding children since I was a baby myself.'

Robert Fraser was impressed by this speech. He nodded several times and touched his fingers as though counting off particularly satisfying events. 'Right. Right,' he said. 'You're absolutely right.' She noticed that, even sitting, he gave an impression of being very tall, but there was something wrong with his proportions. His shoulders, she saw, were exceptionally thin, narrow too and his long neck rose out of them incongruously. She supposed that college lecturers did not get much exercise and so he had never broadened out. And from what she had seen in the films Americans ate poorly, take-outs and pizzas and milkshakes. They ate popcorn in drive-in movies. His face was narrow too, long, and his nose was slightly beaked. But his eyes were bright and warm and when he smiled they lit up. He wore a sweatshirt that said Notre Dame on the front, tight denim jeans with a slight flare at the end and white sneakers. He looked relaxed and self-assured, exactly as she imagined all Americans looked. Although he was much taller, of course, he reminded Josephine of Al Pacino: the same pointed features, the same living eyes, the same casual grace.

'My mother is old now but my sister is taking care of her. My sister is married to a farmer.' She had a sudden image of what her mother's funeral must have been like: the hearse followed by one or two neighbours; one or two men in grey suits; the priest in his colours praying the empty comfort. She wondered if her mother's corpse smelled of drink, or whether the days in hospital had purged her cells. She wondered if anyone walked behind it, or did they all drive, and was there enough money in her mother's post office book to pay for the funeral. It occurred to her then that the priest had wanted to save her, to take her away from her mother before it was too late, before whatever her mother had that made her a lonely old dirty woman became contagious and she was infected beyond redemption. And yet he brought her back too.

'Have you any brothers?'

'I have one, but he's working in England. He's a priest.'

'We're not religious you know,' Robert Fraser said. 'We don't want Robin raised with any guilt thing or anything like that.'

Josephine smiled. 'I'm not religious myself,' she said. 'I don't believe in God at all.' Robert Fraser smiled his gleaming smile and she smiled back in cosy complicity. They understood each other.

'Well,' he said, 'I guess you have some questions for us?'

She loved the upturn in his voice that made statements seem like questions. It was so American. She thought that it was like living through an episode of *Father Knows Best*. 'No,' she said. 'I can see you're a nice person. I think I'd be happy minding – Robin you said? That's a lovely name.'

He laughed. 'I love it. I just love the way you say that. It's the Irish accent.' He beamed at her for a moment, a row of perfect teeth, a furrow of laughter at each side of his mouth. 'I'll have to run it by my wife, of course. I'll have to think about it, but I guess, I like you. But let's see what Robin thinks.'

He stood up suddenly and went out into the hall calling for Robin. She had time to notice the cardboard packing cases of books ranged along the wall, the transparent rectangle of a slide rule sticking up at one side. One book was called *Mathematical Theory of Probability and Statistics*. She wondered what it meant. The words made her shiver as though someone had rippled a deliciously pointed nail along her side. The author's name was R. Von Mises. All the authors had strange names: V.V. Nalimov; O. Neigebauer. Another book was called *The Anatomy of Mathematics*.

Robin was four years old, fair haired and blue eyed. He came shyly into the room, holding his father's hand tightly and leaning uncertainly against his leg. He studied Josephine with care. 'This is my son Robin,' Robert Fraser said. 'Robin say hello to the lady.' Robin said hello. 'This lady might be taking care of you while I'm at the university and Mom is studying,' Robert Fraser said. 'She'll take you for walks and things.'

'To the beach?' Robin said. Josephine winked at him and said that she might be taking him to the beach. She told him that she was born far away from the beach and she was looking forward to paddling.

'What she say, Dad?' Robin said.

Robert Fraser shrugged. 'He'll get used to the way you speak. His last nanny was from Harlem.'

Josephine did not know where Harlem was but she nodded her head anyway. She had the impression that Robin had learned a foreign language and that Mr Fraser was saying that he would have no difficulty learning her kind of English. She made up her mind to speak more slowly and to use American words.

Robin watched her and she winked and made a long face. The wraith of a smile appeared at the corners of his lips. Then she stuck her tongue out, darting it at him, almost too quick to notice. Robin stared at her and then turned to his father.

'Did you see what *she* did?' Robert Fraser shook his head. 'She stuck her tongue out!' He looked quizzically at his father then

Josephine. 'Do it again,' he said. Josephine's tongue darted at him, a russet reptile appearing and vanishing. He started to laugh and she did it again. Now he was grinning broadly.

She caught Robin by the waist and smiled at him. 'I like your name,' she said. 'Like a little bird.' She pulled him close and he resisted a moment, then smiling broadly he melted and perched himself on her knee. 'We got a place in Maine,' he said. 'Real close to the beach.' Josephine said that it sounded lovely. She bounced him a little on her knee and he chuckled and tried to keep his balance, eyes squeezed shut with the effort of concentration.

Robert Fraser watched them and beamed. 'You got him Josephine,' he said. 'He loves sitting on his Mom's knee.' Suddenly Josephine flicked her legs apart and Robin slipped and squealed and she caught him deftly and kept him from falling. He laughed delightedly. 'Again?' he begged. 'Do it again Jo?'

'He's perfect!' Josephine said. She tickled Robin under the arms and he squealed and escaped and then came shyly back for more.

Robert Fraser took a deep breath. 'I guess my wife will like you. We generally have the same taste. I'll run it by her on the phone tonight. If she says yes are you OK to start next week?'

'Sure,' Josephine said carefully. She knew it was an American word because she had heard it on television, but Robert Fraser did not seem to notice her effort. 'I'll have to collect my bits in Dr Casey's. I'll be back by Tuesday.'

'Tuesday's fine. I'll pick you up.'

Josephine assured him that Dr Casey would drive her. 'He can't do enough for me,' she said.

'My wife is flying in at the weekend. I guess she'll be jetlagged and all that, but she's got a meeting with her tutor on Monday. She's taking her master's over here.' A sudden silence expanded between them. They looked at each other and then at the child. 'W.B. Yeats, the poet,' he said. He pronounced the word *poet* as though it were something slightly dangerous, of uncertain provenance and possibly subversive.

'Maybe I could take . . . Robin for a walk now. To get to know each other.'

Robert Fraser swallowed hard and looked at his child. Better to take a chance, he thought. She's a nice girl. This is Ireland for God's sakes.

'Why not?' he asked. He smiled weakly. Josephine smiled too. There was no reason why not.

'Come on Robin,' Josephine said. She held her hand out and tilted her head slightly so that she was looking almost sideways at the child. 'Come on and we'll have a little walk.' Shyly the child placed his hand in Josephine's. He looked frankly at her. 'I like her,' he said. 'She smells real nice.'

Josephine laughed. 'And I thinking I'd leave the perfume off for today,' she said, taking the professor of mathematics by surprise with her construction.

'Take care,' he told her. 'Billie is pretty particular about safety.'

'Billy?'

'Mrs Fraser. Billie. She's real hung up on safety and things. You'll see. She'll put protectors on all the wall sockets. Unbreakable glasses, all that kind of stuff. A lot of kids get kidnapped back home too. She lost her brother that way. He just vanished. I guess childhood is a kinda scary place for her.'

'Oh,' Josephine said, 'he'll be safe in Ireland. We're not like that over here.'

Robert Fraser's smile was warm.

They walked down the hill, under the red and green shade of the cherry trees, one every two or three houses, past the neat lawns and shrubberies, the late daffodils hanging their heads. Robin held her hand in his right hand and trailed his left along the iron rail with the tiny veins of lichen. They turned left at the bottom of the hill and there before them was the gleaming sea, the main street of the town and the little park with the bandstand at the seaward end. The breakwater curled its arms around a small harbour, containing what remained of the town's fishing fleet, doomed to extinction by the EEC – three or four battered trawlers nodding companionably to each other beside the pier amid a litter of seagulls and bits of timber. Beyond the harbour the skeletal frames of a funfair that brought families and thugs to the town in summer – the ghostly Ghost Train, the unrolled roller-coaster, the dead shooting gallery.

In the foreground traffic trawled slowly along the waterfront and a few early tourists lounged around on the seats watching the sun and the water – elderly men and women in soft hats taking advantage of special early-season offers to sleep in damp sheets and breathe the sea air.

'Isn't it beautiful?' Josephine said. 'There's no real beach at all, except about a mile further along,' she added, 'but there's loads of sea and the boats.'

Robin squeezed his eyes up tight as though he were compressing the vista into something child-sized. 'I wanna see the boats,' he said.

Josephine looked around nervously. 'I suppose your father wouldn't mind if we were a bit long.'

They watched a trawler loading ice from a long tube that led from a building labelled Ice House, occasional crystals scattering near them to catch multicoloured sunbeams on their different facets. They saw a man sorting crabs in a barrel.

Gazing in open-eyed amazement at the crabs Robin said, 'Gotta go to the bathroom.'

Josephine remembered the concrete bunker of toilets near the bandstand. She thought that Mr Fraser would never forgive her for sending his little boy into that vile place. Her heart leapt when she thought of the trust that he had placed in her. 'We'll have to go back home,' she said.

'Gotta go,' he said. 'Can't hold on.'

'Go behind that lorry,' she said. He looked terrified.

'No way.' She saw that he was bending his knees so that they flexed together, his left hand grasping at the fabric of his trousers.

'Come on so,' she said, catching his right hand and dragging him along the esplanade. He hopped from one leg to the other and snatched at his trousers constantly. Passers-by stared at the twisting child and the furious girl. An elderly woman laughed aloud. One man stopped and stared after her.

At the entrance she pushed him forwards. 'That's the bath-room,' she said. He stood uncertainly in the dark door and looked at the iron gate that was folded back against the wall. A large rusty padlock hung open and slack-jawed on the bolt. The floor was littered with cigarette butts and bottle-tops. A hollow hissing sound came from the interior and a thin stream of water ran out over a green-stained track. Robin looked into the gloom ahead of him, and rubbed his eyes as though to rub the sunlight out of them. 'Can't go here,' he said. 'It stinks.'

'Well,' she said, 'this is Ireland now and not Harlem and you might as well get used to it.'

'I'm going to wet,' he said. 'I know it. I can feel it coming.'

'Jesus Mary and Joseph!' she said. 'Come on.' She caught his arm and led him round the other side to the ladies'. She dragged him in and pushed him into a cubicle, pulled the door out as far as it would go. She heard his full stream hit the water in the bowl and his contented sigh. 'Hurry up,' she told him. 'This is the ladies'.'

When he came out he was grinning. 'We just made it,' he said. She smiled. 'Good boy,' she said.

'I'm gonna like this place,' he said, and for a moment she thought he meant the public toilet. 'Can I go see the crabs again?'

'No,' she said. 'Your father is going to be wondering where we are.'

The light went out in his face and his lips curled in an incipient snarl. Suddenly he looked puffy and wrinkled like a collapsing balloon. She caught his hand firmly and pulled him up the hill, his slowing steps a dead weight behind her. He repeated over and over that he wanted to go see the crabs, but he did not cry and Josephine was thankful not to be dragging a wailing child past the manicured lawns and gleaming windows. I'll straighten you out, she thought. When I start work. She thought of the perfect fracture that was growing between her childhood and now. Dr Casey's was the first break. And her mother's death would be another. And now she was to live in a new town, with a new family, minding an American child. They would know nothing about her past except what she chose to tell them.

THIRTEEN

'I dreamed I saw the knights in armour coming,' the radio sang, the high-pitched dreamy voice eerie in the warm fug of the car. The windscreen wipers swashed heavily from side to side and the heater fan hummed. The driver tapped the wheel in time to the song. He was hunched forwards slightly, staring through the distorting water at the oncoming lights. Josephine watched him out of the corner of her eye. When the song finished she said, 'That was what's his name. Neil Young. "After The Gold Rush".'

'Is it?' the driver said. He didn't seem interested.

'He's dead,' she said. 'He committed suicide.' The lie pleased her. She looked sideways at the man to see if he noticed but his eyes were fixed on the road. 'He took an overdose.' She wondered what people dying of a drug overdose would look like. Would a stranger know they were dying? Would they have marks? Sores? Scabs? Would they move strangely? She remembered the photographs she had seen of Janis Joplin, the frank angry eyes. And Janis Joplin had taken an overdose.

The man snapped back suddenly and pushed his head against the headrest as though trying to loosen something. 'Jesus,' he said. 'Would you think there was that much rain in it.' He put his hand to his neck and pinched the skin there. Then he slammed his hand back on the wheel and crouched forwards again. 'The lights are no good even,' he said. 'It's too heavy.'

Ahead now they saw a blue strobe and several smaller orange lights. The car in front slowed, its brake-lights suddenly emerging from the submarine gloom. Lights going the other way were moving off fast. Rain jetted from their tyres and their wipers threw great swathes of it on to the road. When they came alongside the wreck they saw that two cars had ploughed into a third skewed across the road, its passenger side caved in, the engine crumpled backwards, the frame of the windows wrinkled like a child's soft toy. They could make out a figure slumped in the driver's seat, androgynous, slightly shapeless. In the glaring light of the strobes sheets of rain were illuminated, pulsing in on top of the figure. A man in a yellow jacket was leaning in the window talking. Another stood by the open door of a squad-car on the far side of the road. He had a radio mike in his hand, the umbilicus coiling back into the darkness of the interior.

Josephine thought: someone else's doctor will be here, racing through the rain to this accident. She thought of herself as in a foreign country although it was no more than thirty miles. 'I'll drive you down of course,' the doctor said. Josephine said that she had arranged a lift. 'No no, I won't hear of it.' But he caved in finally because she would be leaving when he was in surgery. 'I'll be fine,' she said. 'A lady friend is giving me a lift.' He waved goodbye from the surgery window. He had forgotten to ask where her new house was. No forwarding address. No more phone calls from priests. And then she stood at the side of the main road with her thumb out, hoping that there was no emergency to call him out, that he didn't pass by, that someone would stop soon. At the same time she was elated, aware for the first time of a feeling of triumph. The colours of the passing cars seemed to her to be more intense, the sounds they made clearer than ever before. A bird flitting on a tree across the road was a tiny but distinct presence in her consciousness. She wondered at herself.

The driver rolled his window down and called to a Garda who was directing traffic from the middle of the road.

'Anything I can do Sean?'

The Garda looked at them and shook his head. 'Ambulance and fire brigade on the way,' he shouted. 'We'll have to cut her out.'

'All right Sean,' the driver said. He waved his hand and wound the window up. Even in that short moment the right side of his jacket was wet. He cursed under his breath.

Then as they accelerated away the rain stopped. It was as though a line had been drawn across the country, cutting the road five hundred yards beyond the accident. First there was downpour and then there was clear air, the darkening evening sky, the warm tail-lights of the cars in front. The car emerged through it like a swimmer coming up from very deep down. The distant low ridge emerged out of it, and the sea showed beyond the trees on their left. They passed a couple walking on the verge and she had a handful of some kind of pink flowers. The man had his sweater tied around his shoulders, the sleeves knotted across his chest. The ground was dry.

'That was a bad one,' Josephine said.

The man nodded.

'Children?' Josephine asked, jerking her thumb by way of explanation at the blue and pink baby-seat in the back. The man looked at her and then looked back to the road.

'I suppose so,' he said. 'He's four now. He doesn't need the seat. But I never bothered to take it out.'

'That's the way,' she said.

'His mother'll want it anyway, I suppose,' he said. 'She has a car of her own.'

The radio belted out a dreary country and western ballad about a man in a bar-room looking at a women that he knew would sleep with him. Josephine never bothered to remember anything about country and western. She wondered if the Frasers would like that kind of thing. Perhaps Americans did.

'You mightn't think it,' the man said, 'but I'm a real softie. I just can't get rid of that chair.'

Josephine said that was natural.

The man nodded. When he picked her up, her three brown suitcases stacked behind her on the hard shoulder, he thought she might be lively, keep his mind occupied. Within minutes of having her in the car he knew he had made a mistake. She was like a dark piece of furniture that absorbed light in a room, except that she absorbed sound. Conversation fell into her and vanished. He gave up after a few miles. By then he knew that she was going to a new job and that the third suitcase, with which he had almost put his old rugby injury back in action, was full of magazines that she collected. She did not offer any further information and he had been drawn into obstinacy by her reticence and had offered none himself. Normally he was chatty with hitch-hikers.

They were coming into the outskirts of the town. 'Where can I drop you?'

She considered a moment. 'Do you know the bandstand?'

'I do.'

'That'd be grand.'

'That's right on my way,' he said. 'But are you sure you'll be all right there? It's getting dark now.'

'Oh,' she said absently, 'I'll phone the family and they'll collect me.'

He began to indicate and moved into the left-hand lane.

The sea was on that side, glassy flat after the cloudburst, a steel-grey sky suspended above it, cantilevered by denser lower stretches of cloud. A flock of seagulls made a garish white splash against its leaden face. The first seaside bed and breakfasts came into view, then the houses thickened, occasional terraces with Georgian fanlights and foot-scrapers. Then the open expanse of the waterfront, the little park with the battered bandstand, the sweep of the harbour and the trawlers.

He stopped the car and got out to help her with the bags. The light in the boot worked for once and when he dragged out her second bag he saw the bulging pleated anorak that his wife had refused to take when she walked out. It looked obscurely childish, pathetic. 'That child'll never wear that rubbish again,' she said. 'That was all your taste. Frigging St Bernard.' What hurt most was that she didn't love their son Barry and she never had. She had nursed him assiduously according to the best principles of La Lèche, fad-of-the-day at the time, but there was never anything maternal about it. Then when she became a vegetarian Barry did too, vomiting green purée on to a coarse linen bib. Then she became a potter and Barry learned to express his inner self by moulding shapeless lumps of red clay. Along the way there was yoga, several kinds of dietary supplement and a counselling course that qualified her to listen in on other people's screwed-up lives.

A man passed them, a tiny dog straining on a leash. 'Good evening,' the man said. The words were strangely formal.

He slammed the boot and stood staring at it for a moment. The man had stopped and was looking back at the girl and the suitcases.

'Are you going to be all right?' the driver asked.

Josephine gave a tight little nod and said that she was fine.

'I don't mind giving you a lift to their house,' he said. The stranger was moving away, the dog sniffing the rim of the path as though following a trail. There was something odd about his strained waddling walk, his faded Aran cardigan, the high polish on his shoes.

'You're blocking the traffic,' she said. She nodded in the direction of a car trying in vain to change lanes in order to pass them. 'Your man is annoyed.'

'Well, cheerio so,' he said.

As soon as he sat into the driver's seat he felt like hitting himself for saying it. It was his wife's word. In fact it was the last thing she had said to him in person. All their conversations since had been terse and practical, and over the telephone. She had been getting into the battered Toyota. The window was partly rolled down. Barry was sitting in the back seat looking bewildered and clutching the crop-eared teddy bear that he always took to bed with him. 'Cheerio Mike,' she said. Just that. The Toyota revved and pulled out into the Avenue and she was gone for ever. She was taking Barry because it would hurt him.

That bastard that she had taken up with could hardly hide his dislike for the child.

Josephine Strane waited for almost an hour before she saw a taxi. She waved frantically to it and the taxi-driver, seeing that she was alone and had luggage pulled over beside her, rolled down the passenger window.

'Sorry love,' he said. 'Got a fare. Be back in about ten minutes, OK?'

Later, in the warmth of the taxi she told him all about her trip. They were caught in a narrow street that climbed the hill above the town. Ahead of them a JCB was routing out a long narrow trench and a delivery lorry was trying to reverse out of the too-narrow roadway.

'I got a lift from a guard,' she told him. 'A detective I'd say. He was in plain clothes.' She thought about the moment she knew he was a policeman, when he had called to the traffic cop to ask if there was anything he could do about the accident. 'I spotted he was a cop, of course,' she said. 'I seen his gun, stuck on to his hip like you see in the films.'

'Oh Jaze,' the taxi-driver said, 'Special Branch so. The heavy brigade.'

'I had him spotted a mile away.' But he wasn't very intelligent. She had lied to him about Neil Young, that he had committed suicide, and he never noticed.

'You're a sharp one.'

'I keep my eye open. My last employer was a doctor. You get into the habit of keeping your eye open.'

The taxi-driver began to whistle through his teeth and then interrupted himself to say, 'Shagging Urban District Council. They can't leave well enough alone. Digging up every bloody road in sight. Look at that!' The JCB was reversing after the delivery lorry, the driver whirling the wheel furiously, trailing an angular claw that swung wildly to left and right like a wrecker's ball. 'That knacker is going to take the head off someone.'

'It doesn't pay to let the cops know your business,' Josephine said, almost to herself.

'What's that?' the man asked. But she did not reply.

The JCB reversed up the street and swung backwards into a gateway and the traffic moved on again, cars passing the open ditch with care, pedestrians skirting the mud.

'There was someone killed in that smash you were telling me about,' the taxi-driver said as the car swung into the road where the Frasers' house was. 'Some woman.'

'I thought there was,' Josephine said. 'They said the fire brigade would have to cut her out. That's bad.'

'I heard it on the local radio just before I picked you up.'

'I knew she was dead. I could see it.' Josephine smiled happily and settled her hands together in her lap. 'I seen it before.'

The taxi-driver looked at her in his mirror. 'Bit young aren't you love?'

Josephine smiled again. 'The little girl I was minding last time died of meningitis. I found her in the bed. She was just lying there staring up at the ceiling and her skin was all bruised and blotchy. There was a fly walking around in her mouth.'

The taxi-driver made a sharp coughing-spitting sound, covering his mouth with the flat of his hand, and the car pulled into the footpath, one wheel riding up, and lurched to a stop. He covered his shock with a fit of coughing that Josephine knew was false. She got out and took her bags out on to the paving. Then she stood at his door while he radioed in that he was free again.

'Three eighty,' the man said. Josephine counted out the coins. 'The lads say it was some doctor's wife,' he said. 'They had the name and all there now on the radio but I never heard of her. They said she must have been doing a hundred. Dead on admission.' He pulled off the kerb, his rear bumper grating.

Josephine turned her back on the road and looked up at the Frasers' house. There were lights on upstairs but none downstairs. She straightened her shoulders and thought about the boxes of books on the bare floors and the golden-haired boy, a kind of ideal model of an American child. 'This is going to be perfect,' she thought. 'Just perfect.'

FOURTEEN

He had a way of putting his head on one side when he was thinking that made him look just like a robin. And he was cocky too, cheeky, but lovable. And, just like a robin, he would gravitate towards whatever was happening and stand watching it, head canted, concentrating. When Robert Fraser told Billie that he was starting a vegetable patch down at the end of the long narrow garden, Robin perched on the kitchen sink to look out at the place. Evening had settled down between the old walls and a thin fog was manifesting itself. 'Greens?' he said. 'Yuck.' But everyone could see he was interested by the idea. The next day he was beside his father digging with a half-moon edging tool for a shovel. He came in covered in mud and Billie Fraser laughed and hugged him, but Josephine only thought of the trouble of cleaning the clothes.

When Billie Fraser went shopping he tagged along, hoping to pick up something interesting on the way. He became a favourite among the boutiques and supermarkets. Old ladies stopped to tousle his hair and checkout girls gave him sweets. They loved his cheeky response to simple questions. 'What brings *you* in here Robin?'

'Mostly the bus.'

'Ask a stupid question,' they would say, laughing at themselves and at his audacity with words and ideas.

His parents adored him. 'Robin is pretty sharp,' his father said frequently. 'I predict he'll get by in this world without too much trouble.'

'Not if he follows you into Math,' Billie Fraser said, her big laugh bubbling up. 'He should be a doctor or a lawyer or an accountant if he's got brains. That way he won't end up teaching number theory.'

She spoke about Robert Fraser's course as if it were the dead end of all dead ends, the kind of course that people took only because they had no other option. It was a standing joke between them. And then there was Robert Fraser's book which he had been working on since before Robin was born. It would be a university textbook. Once when Josephine was tidying the papers on his desk she read the introduction. Even though she did not understand any of it she was entranced by the names: Archimedes, Euler, Fermat, Gauss. It seemed to her that Robert Fraser knew all these people and they were like casual friends who would drop in when he needed to consult. It was a magical world of complicity and connivance where one name supported another or conspired to deny a third some necessary approbation. It made her feel lonely. And there were the magic symbols of his trade, the squiggles and lines and dots, the foreign letters. Looking at them she felt the weight of incomprehensibility. She thought that people like Robert really understood the world and expressed their knowledge in this secret code. She was permanently excluded from ever understanding things because none of it, not the world itself nor its reflection in his numbers, made any sense to her. There were times when she felt like ripping the pages out and burning them, or scoring them with the sharpened pencil he always used to write. Then she would fold her hands and turn away, holding them tightly to her chest, not trusting them to be free.

But Billie Fraser made fun of it, calling it his magnum opus and saying that when it was written no one would want to read it. She said the writer of a textbook was like a dentist, necessary but never popular. It made him laugh, which Josephine could not understand. She was hurt for him and resented Billie Fraser's joke. But he simply shrugged his shoulders and gave her that magnificent smile. Sometimes they hugged joyfully; and they were not afraid to kiss in front of her. It made her feel as if she were watching a movie sometimes. She would stand near the kitchen sink, at just the right place that allowed her to see down the hall, and when Robert came in Billie would be waiting for him. They would kiss passionately and sometimes their hands would travel up and down. Robert loved to knead Billie's bottom. Sometimes he would catch it in both hands and pull it towards him. She stuck her fingers in his hair like a comb and seemed to tug at it gently.

Then Robert would toss his briefcase on the floor beside the hall table and they would both go to talk to Robin. Billie was at home more often in those early weeks, her classes still organised in a tentative way, and once Robert was settled down with the child she would join Josephine in the kitchen. She had put up a pine shelf over the kitchen bin and filled it with cookery books. Josephine enjoyed riffling through them, studying the beautiful coloured photos that accompanied the text. She loved the organisation, the display, the alternating colours and textures, the simplicity of the designs. Sometimes when Billie came in they would pore over the books together selecting something new and Josephine would prepare it, with Billie's help, Billie converting the American measures into pounds and ounces for her, approximating vegetables and seasonings that were not available on this side of the Atlantic.

Robert often put problems to Robin. It was one of their games and Josephine liked to watch them working on something, perhaps pacing it out on the varnished deal boards of the sitting room. 'Now suppose this frog,' Robert would say, 'was a pretty good jumper, right? Suppose he was absolutely accurate.'

'Absolutely accritt,' Robin would repeat, cocking his head on one side and thinking about it.

'Dead on. OK? He says to himself: I'm gonna jump exactly half the distance to the edge of the pond.'

'Why?'

' 'Cause he's the first frog in the history of the world to have a mathematical turn of mind. This frog is a genius and he wants to do things the hard way just to make it interesting.'

'Frogs are dumb.'

'Not this one.'

'How do you know?'

'Look Robin, we're just supposing, right?'

'Aw, I thought this was for real.'

Then Robert would start all over again: the frog jumping half the distance to the edge of the pond, then half that distance again, half again and so on. How long would it take the frog to get to the shore? Robin would scratch his head and count on his fingers and eventually give up. Then his father would pull the magic answer out of the hat, his face a triumphant grin. 'Never! That frog would never reach the shore because there'd always be half the distance to jump!'

'I told you that frog was dumb,' Robin would say, and the two of them would collapse in laughter on the floor, Robert tickling and Robin squealing.

But hours later he would come back. 'But Dad, that old frog, he'd only be a teeny bit away in the end, right?'

'Yep.'

'He'd be too big to jump half that teeny bit. That frog, he'd get there all right.'

'Robin you got a point there. I guess the frog would have to be real teeny himself.'

'Yeah, but he'd still be too big.'

'You got a point.'

'And if he's so small, how come he's so smart?'

Robert would look with love and longing at his child. 'Sometimes,' he would say, 'small things can be real smart. Like you.'

Billie Fraser had laid down the law for Josephine. There would be no slapping or physical punishment of any kind. If Robin was bad, which he rarely was, Josephine was to explain to him what he did wrong and why he shouldn't do it any more. If he continued to do it, Josephine was to tell Billie or Robert. 'Robin is very bright, Jo,' she had said. 'He understands a bunch of things that kids of his age don't get. If you explain things properly he'll understand why he has to do them.' Josephine had protested that she never used physical punishment on her previous care and she had protested so earnestly that Billie Fraser believed her. 'Just the same Jo, I want you to take special care of Robin.'

Billie Fraser always called her Jo and Robert Fraser soon took up the habit. Josephine did not mind because it seemed to her to be typically American. In the pictures they always had names like Libby and Jesse and Mary Sue, the kind of names that you would never hear in Ireland. She thought Jo was somehow American and modern and she began to tell anyone who asked that it was her name. Jo Strane, working for an American professor and his wife, Robert and Billie. Looking after Robin. When she was away from the house she often saw Robert as a kind of James Stewart: a tall man, shy, an intellectual, like in *Rear Window*. But Billie was not like Grace Kelly. There was no one like Billie.

Grace Kelly was a little chubby and she was a blonde: but Billie Fraser was thin and angular and elegant all at once. She walked loose-limbed like a dancer, moving in several ways. She wore sweaters and T-shirts that showed her full breasts to advantage against the thinness of her body. She wore trousers with tie-downs that ran under her feet – ski-pants she called them – and sometimes she wore denim jeans rolled up at the ends, and a cowboy belt. When she dressed up her suits looked strangely old-fashioned and American. Sometimes she wore white sneakers that were like low boots, reaching to above her ankles and laced up the front. She was so tall that Josephine thought of her as a sally-tree, a willow, young and thin and mobile, blowing with the wind, like the trees that lined the road along by the river at home. Her long black hair had different colours in it whether it was tied up or allowed to drape over her shoulders – just like the leaves of the sally that were dull in calm but flashing white and silver-grey in wind. And, of course, Grace Kelly was younger. Josephine thought that Mr and Mrs Fraser had married late, almost too late to have children, and Robin was the only child they would ever have. There was a danger in that, in the only child. She knew it herself. Spare the rod and spoil the child, that was one of Auntie Mary's. And also, you have to be cruel to be kind. But her mother had never spared the rod.

And Mrs Casey had had osteomyelitis when she was a child and it had left her slightly lame but that must have made her more attractive to Malone the solicitor. But you couldn't punish an adult. Dr Casey could not lock her up in the house or hit her. Only the police could do that and the police took no interest in family matters.

'Now you have to learn a whole new attitude to safety,' Billie told her. 'Back home in the States we're very progressive about this. I guess people in Ireland are still a bit careless about things. Anyway, I'm going to give you these books and you can study them and you'll soon get the idea. In the meantime, let me draw your attention to those socket caps.' She pointed at the new white covers that had been placed over every power socket. 'The idea is that he can't get his finger in the socket. Every time you use an appliance – the vacuum cleaner or the iron for example – we want you to replace the cap. OK? There are other things I'll be talking about later, but for now I want to talk about taking him outside.'

She laid down a series of rules. Robin had a harness with a long leash and she was to use this at all times. She was never to leave the leash out of her hands. If he needed to go to the bathroom she must accompany him at all times. He was to ride in the baby seat at the supermarket and she was not to let him wander off by himself.

'Back home we've got a major problem with child abductions,' she said. 'It happens a lot. Supermarkets are especially dangerous, I guess because the mother or whatever is distracted and thinks it's safe for the child to run around. Don't be fooled.'

'My mother had a harness for me when I was a baby,' Josephine said. She remembered being tied to the leg of the table on a long ribbon of cotton. Later her mother tied her to the bed. That was in the bad time when her mother was often in her room making strange animal sounds and hammering on the furniture. She was drinking heavily then too and she would come into Josephine's room and lecture her on evil and danger. 'Don't go out in the dark,' her mother would say. 'There's strange men looking out for children like you. They'd do things to you. I know. Don't ask me any more. The devil loves the dark, that's the time he comes out. You'll meet him at the corner of Paddy Black's Hill.' She would laugh at that. 'That's where the devil is around here. And if any man asks you to go behind a bush with him don't do it. Men are animals.' Josephine thought of the animal sounds her mother made in her room. Her mother tied her to the bed one night, one hand and one leg. 'You stay there my lassie,' she said. 'I don't want you snooping around tonight. If I find the knots are opened in the morning I'll flay you alive.' It was that night that Susan came and Josephine had cradled her with her free hand, burying her head in the doll-smell and the smooth fabric of her face. And when she came to the Frasers' house the first thing she did was take Susan from the case and put her on her shoulder and say, 'There there pet. There now,' patting her on the back and walking her around the room. The doll's eyes opened and closed with each step through some slight imbalance in the mechanism in her head, and Josephine Strane held her tight because of the vicissitudes of the journey and the uncertain future. Then she placed her on the bed and arranged her limbs and head to her best advantage, and smoothed her dress and hair. She thought there would never again be a man to bring her gifts, no more binding and beating, no animal noises in the darkness.

Then Josephine thought that she had absolute responsibility for the boy while he was in her care. She imagined that his great beauty and his lively personality made him especially vulnerable. Anyone who wanted to abduct children into slavery would be delighted to get Robin, she thought. It would be her personal duty to save him from that. When she thought of the abductors she saw them with faces that she knew, some stubbly, some shiny, full of winks and nods and curious ingratiating tics, hair slicked back with Brylcreem, winkle-toed slip-on shoes scuffed at the edges, owners of darkened cars whose engines hummed and emitted pale steam into the red glow of their own brake-lights.

FIFTEEN

Josephine splashed ineffectually in the shallow end. From time to time a great bubble of water indicated that the wave machine was activating and then she would panic slightly, feeling the uprush of current near her legs. It made her think of the time her mother took her to the seaside, a rough pebbly beach with a steep slope and venomous curling waves that trundled in and cracked on to the beach, white water boiling and simmering and withdrawing. Her mother had wanted her to learn to swim but Josephine was terrified of the threatening sea. 'Go on for Jesus sake,' her mother said repeatedly. She said it under her breath, hissing the words so that the family that set up its picnic twenty yards away would not hear. Eventually she took Josephine by the hand and waded with her into the surf. By the time the waves were breaking about her mother's waist, Josephine was drowning in a surf of fear and mysterious undercurrents that threatened to steal the ground from under her feet. The waves were a wall of green topped by a blossom of white beyond which she could see the sky. When at last she was hit square in the face and jerked out of her mother's grip she screamed and swallowed water and felt herself drawn backwards first, dragging her back and legs along the pebbles of the edge; then back out again, as though an immensely powerful animal were sucking her away from the shore. Uncle Jimmy was what she thought of, pulling her legs, dragging her out to where he was. Auntie Mary was right about straightening out. Uncle Jimmy was dead, not in America. Her mother said he was lost at sea in 1943. When her mother caught her hair and jerked her upright beyond the line of surf it took Josephine a full minute to grasp that her mother was laughing.

'Swim now,' she laughed. 'Swim or you'll be drownded by the next one.' But Josephine did not swim. Realising now that the animal would spit her back each time he sucked her in, that the ghost could not hold her legs, she set herself grimly to the task of frustrating her mother. When she emerged an hour later, blue and chattering, red-eyed from the scouring salt and sand, her mother had admitted defeat.

'You're useless all right, there's no doubt about,' she said. 'I don't know where I got such a fool.'

Although the warm waters of the leisure centre pool were guaranteed shallow, Josephine was reluctant to abandon herself to their invisible strength. Across the way, in the deep pool, the members of a swimming club went up and down marked lanes, breaching and blowing like purposeful whales, and a young man of about her own age swam inelegantly in the unmarked part.

Josephine remembered that there had been a young man on the beach that day too. He came down whistling from the fields that backed the beach, a towel around his neck, his togs in his hand. He changed twenty yards away from them. She remembered the scrupulous care with which he tied the towel around his waist and removed his trousers and underpants. He looked like a man in a skirt, his hairless pimply chest an oddity. When he took the towel away she could see the lump of his thing in the nylon togs. He ran down into the waves and launched himself out into an explosion of water. He swam far out beyond the breaking waves and then rolled on to his back and swam over and back across the beach several times. When he came out he looked cold and his skin was white and she noticed that the nylon was nearly flat, the thing shrivelled by the cold she supposed. She wondered did it go back into them like a horse's thing. Once she heard a girl in school say that she touched one. She said she touched it a lot and she liked it. She called it a stick, but Josephine thought it was too shapeless to be called that. That was a long time ago, on the beach with her mother the day she didn't learn how to swim. A lot of things had changed since then.

After a time Josephine lowered herself into the water. She knelt waiting for the bubbling to begin. She kept her right hand on the edge of the pool and watched the jets from which the water flow would come. She became aware that someone was standing behind her because she felt a shake of drips on her hand. When she looked up she saw that the young man was drying himself vigorously and watching her at the same time.

'How's it going?' he said.

'Fine, thanks.'

'You're scared shitless, aren't you?' He smiled, removing any suggestion that the crudity was intended as an insult. Josephine decided that she might as well admit it.

'I'm afraid of water. I nearly drowned when I was young.'

The young man let his look wander over her and she felt suddenly the extravagance of that expression. 'When you were young,' he repeated.

'When I was small,' she said, suddenly irritated. She wished he would go about his business, finish his drying and change and go home. But instead he threw his towel on to one of the green plastic deckchairs that stood in cosy groups all around the pool and climbed into the pool beside her.

'You're going the wrong way about it,' he told her. 'You have to learn to float first. If you can float you can swim, that's all there is to it.'

'I'm only relaxing,' she said. 'I'm not learning to swim.'

He laughed. 'You can say that again.'

He hunkered down in the pool and stretched his legs out in front of him and suddenly the jets were pumping water in, seven rivers of bubbles like torpedo tracks, meeting in the centre, boiling up. She held her breath and waited. In time the turmoil subsided, but before it ended she had become fascinated by the young man's reaction. He had spread his legs wide so that two of the jets played along the inside of his thighs, and he stared down at them, his face full of childlike glee. Josephine was surprised by the naked pleasure in the face. When the bubbling stopped he looked up at her and laughed.

'Fantastic!' he said. He rose to his feet suddenly. 'Come on. I'll teach you. Anyone can float.'

'I don't want to,' she said, but she did and he knew it. She saw it in his eyes, his willingness to take control, his determination. When he took her palms and led her out into the centre she felt suddenly surrounded, as though someone had placed a warm wrap around her shoulders.

'Now first you have to sit back and let your head go backwards into the water. I'll stand here.' He moved around behind her and she felt the palms of his hands against the side of her head. 'Back. Back. That's it. Further.'

As she leaned backwards she felt the water level rising at a slope along her back and up her neck. She felt it lapping into her ears and spilling down the whorls into her brain. Fear flooded through her and she was suddenly floundering, panicked, trying to get upright from a near-lying position, splashing wildly. 'Easy

easy,' he was saying as if she were a horse he was trying to control. When she stood up she put her hand to her head and her face and was amazed that they were mostly dry.

'You nearly drowned me,' she scolded him.

He was laughing. 'God you're a bad case,' he said. 'I don't know what I'll do with you.'

'It's none of your business anyway,' she said and began to wade towards the edge.

'Don't give up yet,' he said softly. 'We'll try again.'

'We will not,' she said. 'I've better things to do with my time.'

He did persuade her and this time he made her lie back on to his hands. 'I'm going to put my hand on your bottom,' he said apologetically. 'To hold you up. You won't mind.'

'Indeed I will,' she said, but she did not stop him. He held her up by a hand under her neck and another at the top of her thighs and she floated amazingly, feeling only the delicate pressure of his hands and the tiny lapping of the water against her skin. Her legs and hands, stretched out on either side, felt weightless. She stared at the steel girders that held the roof up and imagined that gravity had loosened its hold on her and that she would float slowly out of the water and drift among the roofbeams, touching softly, a lost balloon. Water flowed in and out of her ears and in the intervals between waves she became aware of a faint music filling the vast space between the water and the steel roof. She listened acutely and recognised the sound. She looked up at the young man's anxious face and said, ' "Daydream Believer". The Monkees. 1967.'

He stared down at her, taken by surprise. His mouth opened and closed twice and she laughed. 'You look like a fish,' she said. She saw that his eyes were very direct, looking at her, at whatever he wanted to see. He did not look away when she looked back. There was a red patch on either side of his nose and she guessed that he wore glasses, sometimes anyway, maybe reading glasses. But he did not need them for swimming. He was looking down at her and she knew he could see her even without glasses. It was uncomfortable.

But she floated half-in and half-out of the water and occasionally heard the music and his words and her legs and hands felt almost weightless.

But when he took his hands away the old fear breached her calm and she was struggling with her mother in the boiling surf again. She sank and spluttered, then stood and spat and stared at him like a sullen child while he giggled uncontrollably.

'God,' he said, 'there's no doubt about it you're in a bad way.' She turned and stormed out of the pool and back to the ladies' dressing room.

But when she emerged later he was waiting for her, dressed in a neat sweatshirt, corduroy trousers and clean white trainers. He carried a soft green bag in his left hand. When she came through the swing doors he stood in her way deliberately and smiled. 'I'm sorry,' he said. 'I wanted to tell you to your face. I shouldn't have laughed. I know what it's like, you see. I'm afraid of flying. You know the place where the plane starts to accelerate and you're pushed back into your seat? I always have to get out the sick-bag just in case. I never know.'

She nodded her head sympathetically.

'I love travel but I hate flying, that's the truth of it. So I should understand you being afraid of drowning. Did you have a bad fright or something when you were a kid? That's often the case.'

'I was never in a plane,' she said.

'Let's have a pint,' he said.

'I don't drink.'

'But I do,' he joked, 'and you can watch me. You get a lemonade free with the performance.'

'I hate drunks.'

'God you're a hard one altogether. You're against water and you're against alcohol.' He punched her gently in the arm and winked. But she was in consternation. She shook her head twice. 'I'm only frightened of swimming,' she said. 'That's the only kind of water.'

'Ah come on,' he said, taking her by her left arm and leading her towards the door. 'I'd murder a pint this very minute.'

Later, when she came home, closing the front door as quietly as possible, Billie and Robert exchanged knowing glances and called her in. 'Where have you been till this hour my lady?' Billie said. Robert laughed aloud and said, 'Out with it now. Who's the lucky man?' Billie said, 'Stop it Robert, don't be so nosy.' Then she said, 'Go on Jo, did you meet someone?'

Josephine looked into their eager smiling faces and nodded her head twice. Billie sat up straight on the couch and clapped her hands. She folded her legs up under her, tucking them in and holding one foot with her palm. Robert put down the book he was reading and took his glasses off, folding them in that strict sequence he always followed, first the left arm then the right, then place them face up on the table looking away from him. There was a brief expectant silence, then Billie said, 'I told you, didn't I? I said if you went to that leisure centre you'd be certain to meet someone. I was right.'

'I guess you were, dear,' Robert said. 'But it must be a pretty remote chance. That always fascinates me. Given the factors involved, the night, the time, the whole random nature of the thing, the chemistry even, good God, why the odds are incalculable that the right two people would even be in the same city. It's a chaotic system. And still it happens. It happens all the time. I mean, for God's sake, evolution is so *improbable* when you come to think about it.'

His voice trailed off as he became aware that they were staring at him. 'Thank you for sharing that with us Robert,' Billie said sternly. 'Now let's get down to facts. What's he like Jo? Come on over and sit down right here.' She patted the couch. 'Oh,' she said, 'I was so right about getting you a membership.'

'You're either right or wrong dear, you can't be *so* right.' He chuckled and put his hand in his cardigan pocket.

'Shut up Robert. Go ahead Jo. What was he like? Was he tall dark and handsome?'

Josephine thought carefully about Alan Wallace. 'He works for an electronics company,' she said. 'He's staying up at the hotel. The Bayview. He's nice.'

'I thank God for him,' Robert said. 'Ask him if he has any stuff? I'll take anything.'

'Robert!'

'He's going to teach me to swim,' Josephine said, her eyes shining.

Billie looked at Robert and the same glance flashed between them. 'I think that's just wonderful,' Billie said. 'Now I'm going to make you a cup of chocolate and you get off up to bed. Are you seeing him tomorrow night?'

'Yes. But I'll be home early. I got delayed tonight.'

'Oh don't be silly. Robin is asleep and they're your nights off. We wouldn't mind if you didn't come home at all, would we Robert.'

'Definitely not. We'd be gratified that you were doing your bit for chaos theory and Charlie Darwin's evolution.' He had been discussing probability in relation to evolution with some students yesterday. Why had he been surprised that one of them was a Creationist? Did he think that America had the monopoly? That there wouldn't be literal-minded Catholics?

As she climbed the stairs Josephine heard Billie say, 'Don't rag her so much Robert. Just because she doesn't understand the words doesn't mean she doesn't get the tone. She'll be hurt.'

'But I *like* her dear,' Robert said. 'And I talk like this to everyone.'

Billie Fraser stood at the window of Robert's study. A scatter of paper on the desk covered with various squiggles represented some obscure speculation or the rough-work notes for his next lecture. She had learned that she would tidy them at her peril. Her own notes were always arranged and labelled, a tidy thinker, Yeats and his myriad relationships slowly banking up into a manageable card-index. Sometimes she wondered if the great achievement of American scholarship would be to reduce all of literature to a card-index. She had the feeling that her thesis would be a catalogue, affording only stereotypical glimpses of the poetry.

Below her was the sunlit stretch of road, mottled with leaf-shade, through which her beloved son moved like a bird, darting from cover to cover, followed at a slight distance by Josephine Strane. The child was happy, she thought. The change from the States to here had not been such a great upheaval and she knew that Jo Strane was part of the reason for that.

She marvelled at it. Jo Strane was a nondescript creature, a kind of forgettable kid-next-door in her worn duffle coat and faded jeans, her dull hair and her pale skin. Only her eyes were remarkable – a kind of chestnut brown that grew warmer the more you looked at them, the way the inner skin of a chestnut deepened its colour as you watched.

Now she seemed to be playing some hiding game, stalking Robin among the trees of the roadside. Billie Fraser could hear the child's laughter drifting up. Was there a note of nervousness in it? Probably not. Excitement probably.

She was acutely aware of their good fortune in finding someone so fine. When Robert phoned her that day to say that the very first person he interviewed was perfect she had been more than suspicious, conscious of the improbability that Robert would have been the first to point out. Such good fortune seemed unthinkable. But indeed Jo was an unmixed blessing, excellent with Robin, a good cook, a tidy housekeeper. Most of all she was open and affectionate, thawing slowly out of that Irish reserve. The way she held Robin and talked to him, comforted him when he was upset – she was a natural, a surrogate mother who one day would have her own lovable children and would love them to pieces. Besides, she was someone you could be fond of. Billie thought about that. Yes, she was fond of Josephine Strane, fond of the waif. That was how she thought of the girl: a waif, a woman in waiting, a sleeping beauty. One day she would be kissed by a handsome prince and she would wake up to the world. They would lose her then. But watching that awakening would be a joy in itself.

Now Robin was sprinting for the gate of the house, his face contorted in a mask of mock-terror. Josephine was behind him, her hands outstretched, laughing. Her voice carried through the glass: 'Here comes the bogeyman!' The road stretched downhill in the sunlight towards the rooftops of the town and beyond that was the harbour, the island with its lighthouse and the simple sea. Billie Fraser was content.

SIXTEEN

The bandstand was Victorian, crumbling now, the relentless decomposition of everything that faced the sea. Mike Smith walked all round it, wondering why in his eight years in the town he had never before looked closely at it. He should have brought Barry down here to show him the cast-iron pillars, the terraced floor, the beautiful rotting oak ceiling. There were too many should-have-beens. And she had taken them all. He felt a surge of self-pity, noted it with distaste and turned away to look out to sea. The horizon was empty of everything except a bank of dark clouds. It looked like rain and there was something of early winter in the air. In the foreground a boat lay to, a man in her stern gutting fish. Seagulls gabbled like unruly children. The harbour was unusually quiet for that time of the morning, only a child playing in the pebbles near the water's edge. Two men with dogs stood in conversation near the gents' toilet. Further away the gaunt skeletons of the amusement park stood out against a backdrop of water.

He heard the car before he saw it, that troublesome exhaust. It was as though Claire and her lover were advertising their presence with the brutal sound, punctuating the morning. He wondered what bile she would vomit at him this time. Recently, she had taken to blaming him for her infidelity. It began with the usual complaints. He was always at work. He was away too much. It had progressed in increasingly bizarre increments: he was a fascist cop; he was a soulless philistine; he hated everything that was good on the earth; most bizarre of all, he was an omnivore and full of pieces of dead animals. 'So what does your lover do?' he had asked during a rational moment. 'Does he have a job?'

'That's a typical cop question,' she had answered. 'He doesn't have to have a job to do something.' As it happened he was on the dole and trying to make a few bob by making string-puppets. Mike had first seen him standing outside the Londis supermarket jiggling crude figures. The display was not impressive. The passers-by either ignored it or were embarrassed into dropping a few coins into the tin box at his feet.

After that he made discreet enquiries. The man was not 'known to the police' but the council flat he lived in was in an area that they knew very well indeed. 'You're not bringing Barry out there,' he told her. 'Clear off yourself with your bloody puppeteer, but Barry stays here.'

'You can't look after him,' she said. 'He needs a mother not a policeman. Besides, if you try to hold on to him I'll take it to court. You know very well the way it goes. I'll win.' And the truth was he was due in Dublin for a conference in the morning and he couldn't imagine the organisation and coping involved in finding a baby-sitter. And the other truth was that the woman would always get custody unless he could prove that she was an improper mother, an addict or an alcoholic or deranged. She was none of those things. She was cool, educated, articulate, attractive even if you discounted the clothes she wore. She would be persuasive and she would keep the puppeteer out of sight.

The Toyota pulled into the bus-stop and Claire got out. She opened the back door by leaning her backside hard against it and jerking the handle at the same time. Then she and Barry came towards him. She was holding Barry's hand very firmly, he could see that, as though to prevent the child from running. There was a sense of imbalance, of latent energy in their linkage, as though one slip and the child would tilt forwards into irresistible motion, career across the pavement and launch himself at his father. But they came on steadily. The puppeteer's mistress, he thought. The hippie and the child. The vegetarian. He realised he had begun to think of her in these generic terms a long time ago.

'Here he is,' she said. She let go of the child's hand and he stood there uncertain of what to do. 'You have an hour. We have to do the shopping.'

'What?'

'I told you on the phone. He could visit you today.'

With a sick feeling he realised she was playing out some scenario she had read about or seen in a film, the divorcee allowing her ex-husband access. 'You never said anything about it,' he said.

'Well do you want him or don't you?' she hissed. ''Cause I can take him with me if you like.' She had said something like that once, years ago, the first time he met her. 'Well, do you want me or don't you?' The frank invitation was too much for him. He had paid handsomely for the pleasure since then – a failed marriage, a cold house, a cold heart. She wasn't entirely to blame, he knew that, but he had loved her once and that made all the difference between them.

'No,' he said quickly. 'No, I do of course. I'm delighted. Come here Barry. I just thought it would be something else.'

'I don't know what you frigging thought it was,' she said. Her constant use of foul language in front of the child was another way of getting at him, he knew. He rarely swore himself and was especially careful in front of children.

Barry took two paces forwards and stood between them.

'Let's go down and look at the bandstand,' Mike said. Barry nodded.

'Right. Two hours so,' Claire said. 'We'll be here.'

Wintry showers the forecast said. Josephine watched one swing in from the sea, a curtain of grey with a thin line of white at its base. It swept along the breakwater and fell on the town sending shoppers scurrying for cover. It missed the amusement park. It missed the bandstand. Instead it hissed among the ancient peeling trawlers and discarded lobster pots.

All around her wind nicked at insecurities, shivered in the loose awnings, flicked frayed bunting and disturbed the soggy wrappers that littered the ground. The great roller-coaster looked like the beached skeleton of a whale. The boating lake was grey and scrofulous, a few pale seabirds paddling on it. There was water everywhere. New graffiti gleamed wet – Scruffy loves Sonia, Brits Out. A faint smell of vomit and urine emanated from behind the booths. A dog was yapping some-where, rapid sharp barks that seemed to echo the fluttering of small things.

Robin ran between the stiff legs of the Ferris wheel chasing some imaginary prey, face intent, one hand cocked like a gun. She was glad she had brought his anorak, if there were going to be showers like that. She sat on the concrete steps of the Ghost Train and flicked through the gleaming drawing rooms and neat herbaceous borders of *Homes & Gardens*. She smiled as she thought of the system she had developed for getting this and other favourites like *Country Life, Good Housekeeping*. Robin had become obsessed by English comics. She bought him the *Dandy* regularly, and he would spend hours chuckling over the pictures of Desperate Dan and the Bash Street Kids. Her trick was to stand among the magazines and then send Robin to the counter with his money in his fist. The girls were always charmed by his accent, his cornflower-blue eyes and white-gold hair. His precocious chatter delighted them.

'He's a real old man,' they would say, grinning and nudging each other. 'Listen to the guff out of him!'

'The words he has!'

'Tell us again, Robin,' they would plead. 'Why do you like the *Dandy*?' and Robin would oblige them with some gem of his father's or mother's. 'The *Day*ndy,' he would drawl, 'just goddam British impeeliss prop gander.' It was one of Robert's jokes. They would dissolve in peals of laughter, slapping the counter and supporting each other as though they were likely to slide sideways on to the floor from weakness.

Homes & Gardens fitted neatly inside her duffle coat. She liked the firm flatness of it against her belly, the way it worked against her as she moved, the rectangle of sweat that built up under it on warm days. She would hold Robin's hand as she walked out, throwing something over her shoulder to the shopgirls. 'He's a gas man, isn't he?' she would say. Or, 'You couldn't be up to him.' Sometimes, as a cover, she bought something herself, *Scientific American* for Robert or one of the tiny literary journals that flowered and faded by the month for Billie. She never bought anything for herself, but she enjoyed the feeling of mystery her purchases engendered in the staff. They couldn't know who the *Scientific American* was for. Shoplifting, she read in *Vogue* some weeks ago (marvelling that until now she did not know the name for what she did) accounted for as much as ten per cent of all losses in stores. The article detailed the kind of things people stole: watches, jewellery, clothes, ornaments, books. Josephine searched eagerly for magazines and did not find them among the list. She was disappointed, but also intrigued at the variety of things that could be taken. Some of the methods described had not occurred to her and she contemplated the idea of walking out of a shop wearing two pairs of jeans. The idea excited her. Where was the dunce now? she thought. What if the Master knew how clever she had become?

Robin had wandered off among the derelict arcades and she could hear his shooting and wounded cries carried on the fitful wind. She put the magazine into her shoulder bag and went to look for him. She went carefully, keeping out of sight, and found him kneeling on a slab of concrete, firing rapidly at something in the distance.

She stayed hidden, watching him, feeling like the camera in those films where a movement betrays the existence of a watcher. Who killed cock robin? she thought. I, said the sparrow, with my bow and arrow. She laughed and flicked her hair, a small birdlike movement. She was light on her feet and dainty in motion: she could move silently and flit behind things. He won't catch me, not Robin. She remembered hiding from her mother in the abandoned escallonia hedge. The plants were so big she could move along inside for the whole length.

'Josephine? *Josephine!* Her mother's legs passing outside, a nylon stocking with a long ladder in it, stretched like a web around her calf. Her mother was no good at finding.

After a time she saw him look around and realise where he was. He got up and rubbed one puzzled eye then set off at a comical trot. He turned right, rounding the side of the closed-down shooting gallery. She followed and saw him emerge in front of the Ghost Train steps. She saw him stare intently at the sign and then down at the steps. He looked uneasy.

Lost, Josephine thought. You're lost child. The bogeyman is coming.

Robin was wondering where Josephine had gone. Consternation was written all over his face. He knew she had been sitting there moments before. He had come back expecting to see her still riffling through her magazine, the flat fawn of her duffle coat blending with the concrete and slime of the steps. Instead the wintry wind ruffled the puddles and a stream of sun threw long shadows at him. There was no Josephine.

He walked up to the steps and pointed at them as if indicating to someone that this is where she had been. Then he looked around, searching each of the sites in turn. He followed the trail of the roller-coaster all the way from its beginning to end. He circled the Ferris wheel twice, as though she might somehow have become stuck in one of the seats high up. They swung empty, squeaking in the wind. The lower ones had been removed. He repeatedly glanced up at the Ghost Train signboard, which depicted a ghoulish wraith looming high over a pair of screaming children, amorphous hands stretched out, the gross embryo of fingers and nails; behind them the shape of a coffin and a fanged man staring at him. As he stood there his face began to lose its shape. The left side of his lip sagged and his eyes narrowed. He joined his hands in front, squeezed them together hard.

Suddenly he began to run. There was no direction to it. He ran first at the Ferris wheel and rushed around the steel uprights. He paused for a moment and looked around again, as if he had become trapped in a maze and sought the way out. Then he was running towards the roadway. Through the underpass that took a side road to a council estate, the walls splashed with slogans and football teams. Arsenal for the cup. Georgie Best. A group of teenagers stepped aside as he passed, guffawing and pointing. They milled about, prancing and squealing in his wake, suddenly more sombre when Josephine passed through. She held her breath, her heart racing, conscious of the walls on each side, the low dripping concrete roof, rather than the open air at both ends, only the width of a roadway apart. When she emerged into the wind on the far side she slowed down. She looked back and thought: *Blackmail*, Alfred Hitchock. The same thing – the bridge overhead, the boys jeering. She spat on to the ground and walked on, her eyes picking Robin from the dusty multicoloured houses of the front.

He emerged on to the roadside path and stared across at the little harbour. He saw the boats gleaming after the rain. He saw the cloud dragging away through the town, cars passing, seagulls following a half-decker past the breakwater. Tears rolled down his face and a monstrous wail emerged. He ran again. This time he ran in the direction of home but soon found himself in unfamiliar streets. Adults pushed by in plastic overcoats. Umbrellas reshaped every view. The rain came down again, a thundering downpour that hopped off the street in little vees and soaked him through his anorak, getting down his neck and making his trousers hard and cold. He stood by a lamp-post crying and suddenly aware of a pressing need to go to the bathroom.

That was how he was when Josephine came out of hiding. She walked up the street and called his name and he turned and saw her and ran to her. She said nothing but took his hand. He wailed a long tale of terror and insecurity and apology and she stared straight ahead and marched him home.

Billie and Robert were both there, drinking coffee, half propped, half sitting on the kitchen presses. Billie had bought a rough wool cardigan at a craft shop the week before. It had a huge bird in the pattern for the back, a reddish-brown eagle or a phoenix, and the same bird was repeated in small on the front. She had it open now, folding the smaller birds away, the sleeves, which Josephine thought were far too long, rolled loosely back. Josephine brought Robin straight in to them.

'He ran away from me,' she said. 'I thought he was gone. He hid on me and then he ran away.'

They stared at her and then at Robin. The child was pale, his lips working as though he had lost control of them, big round eyes full of fear.

'My God he's completely wet,' Billie said.

'He ran away?' Robert said.

'He did. He deliberately ran away. He says he got lost, but I was there all the time. He put the heart crossways in me.'

'She wasn't at the Ghost Train,' Robin wailed. 'She was first and then she wasn't.' Billie bustled him away and soon they heard water running into the bath.

'I got a bad fright,' Josephine said.

Robert said, 'I bet you did. Well, I guess I have to say we're sorry on behalf of Robin. I guess it's a phase. He never did run away before.'

Josephine was shivering. Now Robert saw that she too was wet, her hair straightened by the rain, her shoes soft and noisy. 'Look at you,' he said. 'You're wet right through.' A shaft of sunlight came through the seaward window and instantly the pine table glowed. The rain was a curtain drawing towards the horizon. The whole room was suddenly rich and warm. 'Go dry off,' he told her sternly. 'Take a shower, you'll feel better. Everything is all right. He's safe and he won't do it again. I'll talk to him. You did well. Go on Josephine. Get changed.'

Josephine added that month's *Homes & Gardens* to the pile under her bed. She thought about the featured house – the black and white kitchen, the antique walnut dining table in the contrasting dining room, the glass wall that looked out on a London garden of wild plants rising off nineteenth-century Portland stone. The profusion of the garden was like an antidote to the suffocating precision of the rooms, the studied contrast, the lack of fuss. 'Trading schooners plied from London to the south coast stopping at every port and returning in ballast with best Portland stone,' the article read. 'Mr Wallace used the stone to build this elegant terrace, keeping No. 15, the finest of them all, for his daughter as a dowry. Tucked away behind the stern frontage is a Victorian gem with a history.' The owners of No. 15 had a Victorian-doll collection of which they were very proud. They displayed them in different parts of the house and the photographer's lights sparkled on their ceramic faces.

She was startled out of her thoughts by Billie shouting from the foot of the stairs, 'Josephine there's a young man on the line. Come on down.'

It was Alan Wallace. 'Hi Josephine,' he said. 'I was wondering if you were coming back for another lesson. Up at the pool. I'll be there tomorrow night at seven myself.'

She thought for a moment. Learn your lessons, Auntie Mary used to say, and you'll have something to fall back on. What did that mean? 'I was going to go up then myself,' she said. The girls at school had sniggered when she couldn't recite the times tables, but some of them couldn't do it either. Mocking is catching, that was one of Auntie Mary's.

'So that's all right so,' he said. 'See you.'

'See you,' she replied and hung up.

Billie and Robert were standing in the kitchen grinning at each other.

'Was that a date?' Billie asked.

Josephine blushed. 'I suppose so.'

'Great,' Robert said.

'I told you so,' Billie said.

Suddenly Josephine's face became grim. 'I might have to hand in my notice,' she said. 'If he's going to get notions like that I wouldn't be able to keep going. I got a bad fright when he ran off.'

'Oh no, Jo,' Billie said. 'No, he won't do it again.'

'He might have run under a car or someone might have picked him up. Some dirty old man like we're always hearing about. The country is full of them by all accounts.'

'No, this is Ireland. Remember Jo? Don't take those books I gave you too seriously. This is a nice neighbourhood. I was just worried about general safety. Just not taking risks.'

They shook their heads and assured her that Robin did not behave like that normally, that he must have lost his head for a moment, got caught up in some fool game. They'd talk to him about it. They would be stern. They would punish him by banning his favourite television programmes for a few days.

'It's not easy to mind him,' Josephine said. 'I'm not used to children like that. He has no notion of obedience at all. That's the American way I suppose, but it's not easy for me. And I'm *used* to minding children. Normal children.'

Billie and Robert looked at each other and Robert said, 'I'll go up and talk to him now. Right before he gets to sleep. I'll make him see that he can't just run away.'

But he returned half an hour later looking worn. 'He keeps saying the same old thing,' he said. 'About this Ghost Train and all. I wonder has he got a fever, but he doesn't feel hot. He says Jo just disappeared. That can't be right, can it Jo?'

Josephine was suddenly intense, angry, hard-edged. 'If I told you once I told you a hundred times, he ran away. He's a bold child. He did it on purpose. If you think I'm not good enough I'll leave. There's plenty of other houses that'd be glad enough to get me. When you'll believe a bold child before you believe me, that says it all to me.'

After a time they calmed her and she agreed not to go. She was an ideal person to mind Robin, they said, cool, capable, loving but not afraid to speak her mind. They valued that. They put a premium on honesty. And they were worried, too. Robin was their only child and they had nothing to go on. Perhaps this was a phase all children went through, a seeking after independence, the first steps towards setting out on their own. They would ask among their colleagues since they still had very few acquaintances. Billie said she had met a woman of her own age who was studying psychology. She would be the perfect person to ask.

'I guess our approach to child-rearing is a bit theoretical,' Robert said. 'I mean we've read a few books and things. But neither of us has much in the way of practical experience here. You know a hell of a lot more than us, Jo. We just have to trust you, that's all.' Billie stood at the kitchen window looking out, the eagle or the phoenix or whatever it was looking inwards. Josephine noticed that the craftswoman who knitted it forgot to give it eyes. And they had to have these crooked heavy mugs made in a local pottery instead of proper china. Billie had pointed out the potter's thumb-print under the handle as if it was something admirable. Josephine thought it was disgusting.

'Trust is vital,' Josephine said, remembering as she said it that it was the beginning of an answer to something. She racked her brain for the question and then it came to her. Worried, Hove, said that her husband of six months was out late every night – drinking with his mates he said – and had lost all interest in love. Before he had been ardent in his passion, she said, especially before they were married, but now that he had tied the knot he was losing interest. She wondered if he was having an affair and declared that she couldn't bear it if there was another woman. She still loved him deeply. The answer had counselled trust, time and a more pro-active approach to sex. 'Meet him at the front door in your undies,' the answer said. 'Lure him to the bedroom with chilled champagne and passionate music. Or go away for a dirty weekend.' He probably *was* drinking with his mates on those late nights out because many men found it difficult to adjust to the changes in their lives occasioned by marriage. The answer had ended by emphasising again the importance of mutual trust.

SEVENTEEN

For some reason the amusements were open that night, at least a single street of arcades with one-arm bandits, pinball machines, motorbike simulators, fantasy racing, bingo and ice-cream cones. The wind was gone and the streets were dry, except for the hollow places where water had accumulated, blocked shores and gutters and potholes. They wandered along it arm in arm. They had their swimming bags over their shoulders and their hair was wet, but the night was unseasonably warm, close and airless almost. The arcades pumped out their fairground hits and the saccharine melodies lent a romance to the faded town.

That night Josephine had allowed herself to float on her back for twenty and thirty seconds at a time and had been aware of the delicious sense of release, of yielding that it entailed. Also she had felt the light presence of his hands at her shoulders and thighs and the feeling had not been unpleasant. She lay in the body-warm water in a dream, her mind drifting backwards and forwards. She thought about Jean and Dr Casey and wondered how they were. She thought about the cars at Auntie Mary's funeral and remembered hearing that the driver of one of them had died of a heart attack swimming in Inch Strand. The cold did it, they said. She remembered a rhyme that was said a lot when she was a child: April and May keep out of the say, June and July swim till you die. And Auntie Mary used to say, Never cast a clout till May is out. She remembered her mother yelling at her when she was three or four years old, 'What noise? What noise are you talking about? I'll give you noise,' and catching her by the hair and dragged her to the sink where the water from the dishes was still full, a rime of cold fat and soapy bubbles on the surface. 'You won't hear any fucking sounds down there,' she yelled and shoved Josephine's head into the water. She remembered that her face was underwater but her ears were still on the surface and she could hear her mother muttering about snooping children and people sticking their noses into other people's business. The memory made her laugh and Alan Wallace smiled down at her contentedly.

'You have to let go,' Alan Wallace told her. 'You're too uptight. You have to take chances.'

'It goes against the grain,' she said. 'Minding children makes you careful.'

'There's careful and careful in it,' he said. 'You have to be careful with the child I suppose. But that's work. That's different.'

Later he mocked her carefulness.

'If I was you, I'd be paranoid,' he said. 'You read all about these fellows that kidnap children. They take them away to the Middle East to be slaves to the Arabs. Did you ever think about that though?'

She rose to the bait. 'I'm always worried about it,' she told him seriously. 'I have to keep an eye out all the time. You never know.' She was thinking of Robin's golden head, his blue eyes looking at her in that quizzical way of his. 'What you *doin'*, Jo?' She loved the way he wanted to understand everything. The way he looked up at her with his mouth open, his eyes drinking in her movements. When she hoisted him into the air and nuzzled him he squealed with laughter. She loved the way he came to her and said: 'Play bogeyman Jo?' and the way he ran screaming around the house when she came after him, her arms high above her head, her face contorted. And how he fell asleep sometimes in her arms.

'You never know,' he echoed. 'God Jo, you're so *grown up*!'

By now they were sitting on one of the metal benches facing across the harbour. A heavy soughing swell was running in past the head of the breakwater and lifting and dropping the water and the boats on it in a steady rhythm. He stretched his arm out and encircled her shoulder and pulled her round to face him.

'You're so pretty,' he said, and pulled her face to his. They kissed for a time and she allowed his tongue to come in, feeling it like a pleasant worm in her mouth, insinuating itself into every corner. Soon her own tongue was struggling with his. After a time they stopped and drew breath. When they started again his right hand was on her breast. Josephine grew alarmed and her breathing shortened, but he took it as a sign of arousal and put his hand between her thighs where it pressed ineffectually against the rigid gusset of her jeans.

She pulled away and crossed her legs, staring sideways at a set of headlights winking between the buildings of the waterfront.

'What's wrong Jo?' he asked, obviously puzzled.

'Nothing,' she said.

'Come on,' he said gently. 'What's wrong?'

'All right so,' she said, rounding on him, spitting the words at him. 'If you want to know so, I'll tell you. You're all the same. Boys are all the same. It's always only the one thing. You have to get it. That's all. And when you get it you're off then. One-track minds.'

He shook his head. 'Not like that,' he said. 'I like you Jo. I really do.'

'Huh. If you liked me you'd respect me.'

'I do,' he said. 'But I like you in other ways too.'

She felt her face suddenly red, anger welling up inside. She thought of her mother putting on lipstick, grinning and pouting at the cracked mirror, the knock at the door and her mother's

false voice calling, 'Keep your shirt on, I'll be out in a minute.'
She wondered again who those mysterious callers of her childhood had been, and whether any of them might have been her
father. She was never allowed to see them. 'They like their
privacy,' her mother often said. Or, 'They're shy and they don't
like kids.' Dark suits, shiny shoes, overcoats turned up at the
collar. Only once a smiling face came from the shadow – 'Look
what the nice man brought . . .' – but that was Susan. Sometimes there was a car, its lights dipped, its engine rumbling
quietly. They all had a familiar look, a common shrug of the
shoulders, a way of opening the car door, a way of turning their
toes out and swaying at the shoulder when they walked.
Sometimes she wondered if they were indeed no more than
different shapings of the one person, different incarnations of
the same perpetual mystery. Some nights she was sent to stay at
Auntie Mary's, carrying her nightdress in a cardboard suitcase
through the grey or pitch-black streets. Those nights her
mother sipped from a glass of clear liquid as she touched
her face, scarring herself with rouge, lipstick, mascara. She
held the glass delicately, one small finger crooked outwards like
the stalk of a mushroom. 'Gin makes you sin,' she would say,
laughing and waving an admonitory finger at Josephine. 'Stick
to lemonade.'

'If you do like me,' Josephine said, sliding along the bench
away from Alan Wallace and pulling the front of her duffel coat
around her like a wad of blankets.

'Jo, I do, you know that.'

'If you do, why are you always talking about stealing Robin?'

He laughed first and then saw that she was serious. 'Jo, it's a joke. I was poking fun at you. Taking the mickey. You don't seriously think I meant anything by it?'

'You said yourself there's always people around.'

'You don't think that I – for Christ's sake this is going too far!'

'All right so,' she said. 'You can do it again.'

He stared at her. 'What?'

'What you were doing.'

'Just like that?'

'Well do you want to or don't you?'

He slid along the bench and looked closely into her face. 'Are you serious?' For an answer she leaned forwards and stuck her tongue into his mouth. The music from the arcades was beginning to wind down. Lights were going out.

A police car came slowly along the waterfront and stopped in the nearby carpark. A guard got out and twirled his flash-lamp around. Josephine rearranged her clothes quickly and they stood up.

'Everything all right miss?' the guard said. Josephine giggled and said she was fine.

'Off home so, I suppose?' the guard said, and Josephine said she was off home all right. The guard flashed his torch around the seat and the surrounding bushes then went down towards the bandstand. They saw the flickering torchlight on the iron uprights and the rotting roof. When he came back he waved the light towards them. 'Night so. Safe home,' he called and got into his car and reversed out on to the street. A single arcade was still showing lights. Music drifted out from it. 'Sweet Caroline,' the effeminate voice sang', good times never seemed so good.'

'Sweet Caroline,' Josephine said. 'Neil Diamond.'

She saw a small white dog darting between shadows at the edge of the pier, such a tiny movement that she wondered whether she might be imagining it. She watched Alan stuff the ends of his shirt into his belt. 'I'll be murdered for staying out so late without telling them.'

'Come back to my room,' he said. 'There's a late-night movie on.'

'I saw it already,' she said. 'It's ancient.'

'It's a classic,' he said.

'I hate that Anthony Perkins,' she said. 'I never watch anything with him in it. He's so fake. And anyway, who'd stay in a hotel like that?'

'We wouldn't have to watch the movie,' Alan Wallace said plaintively.

'I'll be murdered if I'm not back,' she said.

That night she found it difficult to sleep, rolling about in hot sheets, floating on a gelatinous fluid that buoyed her up but held her down at the same time, intensely aware of the heat of the radiator under the dormer window. In the end she got up and screwed the valve down tight and opened the window a crack. A suggestion of salt water was borne in on the breeze and the room seemed to be cooler immediately. She climbed back into bed and lay flat on her back, her legs splayed, her hands crossed on top of the sheets, and it was in that posture that sleep overtook her. But sleep was no relief.

She dreamed of Alan Wallace. She saw herself, as if from a secure hiding place, stretched on the seat by the seafront. She heard the breathing of the ocean swells and the thumping and grinding of the trawlers. She could hear her own breathing too, guttural and harsh. She moved unsteadily – a camera – small obstacles passing before her vision: branches, pieces of metal, a frame of some kind. In the camera's unblinking eye she saw Alan Wallace opening the zip in her trousers and exposing her belly. Suddenly she was much closer and could see that the skin of her stomach was wizened, rucked like an old carpet: that her pubic hair, protruding obscenely from the top of her panties, was grey and thin and long, more like an old man's beard. And then she saw him step back and look down at her and a grey-winged seagull flew down and perched on the rim of her jeans and began to peck at her skin. And then she saw that Robin was there, pointing and laughing, his head on one side like the seagull's. The seagull was pulling pieces of flesh that gleamed like mackerel skin and stretching his neck up to swallow them and Robin was almost hysterical with joy. And then the scene shifted so that she was watching Alan walking away. She saw that he wore shiny shoes and that he walked with his feet splayed out, heaving his shoulders from side to side, and that his suit was black. Behind him followed Robin, walking in a trance-like state, his hands outstretched, his face gleaming coldly. She could hear music too, a thin weird piping, but the tune was familiar enough.

EIGHTEEN

'Show me those socks,' Josephine Strane said. 'Don't sneak them into the wash when I'm not looking.' Robin picked them up and held them out. She wrinkled her nose and said, 'Yuck.' She caught them between her index finger and thumb and, holding them at arm's length so that she had to waddle backwards on her haunches, she placed them carefully in the middle of the washing-machine drum. 'You were out in the garden and you got them all dirty. You have to show me everything.' Keep yourself clean all over child, Auntie Mary used to say. 'I'll tell you a saying that we have here in Ireland, whatever about America. Cleanliness is next to godliness. That means you have to be clean to be good.' Robin nodded guiltily and pulled at the back of his trousers. 'Can I go play with my toys now?'

Afterwards she spoke quietly to the boy and asked him to try to keep his clothes clean in future. 'Even in the garden,' she said. 'You don't have to get dirt on everything.'

'Gardens're all dirt,' he told her.

'Don't back-answer me,' she said sharply. 'Just try. That's all I ask. Remember I have to clean after you.'

Mrs Casey's father had brought dirt into the house. 'Dirt brings disease,' she added.

'What disease?'

Josephine folded her arms and glared at him; and then unexpectedly she thought of Susan, her smooth unchanging face, and she knelt and caught Robin, clasped him tightly and rocked him to and fro. He seemed bewildered by her mood, uncertain how to react. Then he began to snuffle into her shoulder. 'There now,' she said. 'There now. It's nothing after all. Only a bit of dirt. You can't help it.'

'I love you Robin,' she thought. Something terrible was going to happen, she knew. She had known it for days now, a steady pressure growing inside her. She was powerless to stop it. She hunted everywhere for the cause, considering every action, looking beyond the surface of things. Everything had a meaning, she knew, not always apparent but there none the less. Robin was the centre of it all. She knew that whatever was going to happen would happen to him and it was her duty to prevent it, but also she knew that she would be in it. She dreaded that she would be the cause, that something in her would trigger the catastrophe. She was irritable with him as a result, loathing herself for it, but unable to prevent it.

She hugged him tighter and his snuffle became a stifled wail. 'You're hurting me!' he cried and shook her hands free.

'Don't you sauce me!' she said. 'You're going from bad to worse. I don't know what your parents will say.'

'I did not sauce you,' he cried, his face reddening. 'I just said—'

She raised a hand and held it quivering behind her, poised to strike. He lowered his head and retreated two steps, holding his hands in front of his face.

'I won't do it,' she cried. 'Even though you're driving me to it with your boldness. I won't break my promise.' Then lowering her hand – 'Get out of my sight. Get up to your room and don't let me hear from you for the rest of the day until bath-time. Go!' She stood up suddenly, uncoiling from her haunches with a strange fluidity, balletic almost, reaching out for him with palms extended. But he wriggled through the door and she could hear his footsteps going away through the house and up the stairs. Presently she heard his bedroom door close.

When the washing machine was running she settled down in front of the television. *The Love Boat* was on, and she watched the complicated relationships, the mixture of mock-formal and mock-casual, the entertainers and the stewards, the officers and the passengers, as though studying for a future career. During the third part the phone rang. She let it ring until it stopped, but it started again and she knew Robin would tell them that she didn't answer it. She got up wearily and turned the sound down.

She knew when she picked up the phone that it was Alan, before she even heard his voice.

'Well?' she said.

'God Jo, I thought you were out,' he said. 'I thought I missed you.'

'No,' she said, coldly.

'Jo? Is something wrong?'

'No.'

'I was thinking about last night,' he said. 'I had to give you a ring.'

Her mind flooded with the image of the seagull, the thin tufted strips of flesh gleaming like fish-skin in the weird light.

'Can you talk? I was thinking about the time we were sitting on the bench. Before the cops came along.'

'I can't talk now,' she said.

'God, you were great,' he said. 'I love you, I think.'

'I can't go swimming any more,' she said, struggling to keep her gorge down. Suddenly her throat was closing, her stomach heaving in great rolling swells.

'Who cares about swimming!'

'I have to go.'

'Wait! Jo! What about Sunday night? I have to go away for a few weeks. The company is sending me on a training course. What about Sunday night?'

'You scratched me,' she said. She didn't know what she was saying, could scarcely concentrate enough to force the words out. 'You scratched and tore me. You're supposed to keep your hands outside. You scratched me. You're a dirty filthy person.'

The other side of the line was silent and she took the opportunity to slam the phone down hard as she had seen it done in the pictures. But instead of ramming the cradles she sent it skittering away across the floor to the extent of its lead, the coils opening out and then springing back so that the hand-piece spun back towards her like a terrier returning to the attack.

Then she called Robin down and roughly forced him into his anorak and tied the harness around him and took up the lead even though Billie had agreed that she did not need to use it any more. She marched him down to the harbour and for a time they threw stones from the little beach, watching them splash into the glassy water, the ripples spreading through the harbour, each distinct ripple decaying as it worked from the centre out until by the time it reached the boats it was indistinguishable. Robin played in the skeleton of a rotten boat in the corner above the high-water mark, her blackened ribs clawing out of the muddy sub-layer, a few strakes of her sides delineated in the weed and mud by darker lines. Then they went out on to the pier to watch the ice being loaded and the behaviour of a man who was chipping rust off a band of metal that ran along the side of a boat. A recent gale had brought pebbles and weed on to the breakwater and Robin picked up a rod of kelp to chase a seagull.

She watched him charging around the pier and swinging the fleshy stalk above his head. She shivered. When he grew tired of the game she made him throw the rod into the water.

'Robin,' she said. 'Promise me one thing. When you go to sleep at night I want you to do something. I want you to keep your hands outside the blankets. Never inside.'

Robin looked up at her with big eyes. 'Why?'

'Because,' she said. 'Because it gives you a disease if you put your hands inside. It makes you rot, like that rotten fish down there.' She pointed down at a dogfish, floating belly-up between the boat and the pier, an albumen-white bubble of flesh torn out of his craw, his back twisted to an unnatural angle. Robin stared down at it.

'You don't want to rot, do you Robin?' He shook his head. 'That's my boy,' she said, smiling broadly. 'Do you want to play on the boat?' He nodded. 'Come on then.'

She led him to the secluded steps that led down to the water. Here they were only overlooked if someone stood directly above them on the quay. They stepped gingerly down the slime-covered steps and she pulled on the rope that brought a small open boat thudding gently against the stones. She unclipped the harness from his chest and Robin climbed in, almost dropping a foot into the water in his excitement, squealing with delight as the boat rocked.

Josephine pushed the boat gently and watched as she coasted to the length of her scope, perhaps ten feet away. Robin explored the seats and bilgeboards, taking up crab shells and holding them up for scrutiny, opened mussels, pieces of dried fish, the rusty bailing can, loose rope. Satisfied that he had exhausted the pleasures of rubbish, he rocked the boat from side to side squealing with delight. A thin film of diesel oil gave the water a glassy appearance, collecting in ornate shapes and refracting light, making the water look active and glowing. Fishermen called to each other across the moored boats and somewhere someone repeatedly pulled the starter cord of an outboard motor – whirring and dying, whirring and dying. The air was dominated by the tartness of a fishing port, a smell combined of oil, salt, fish, timber and wet rope.

Robin was kneeling on the transom seat staring at the ancient grey Seagull engine, an aluminium leg cocked out from the transom. He was muttering happily to himself, wriggling the handle and watching the propeller scooping down into the water and out again as the boat lifted and fell. Josephine backed slowly up the steps. At the top she looked carefully around and noted the smell of frying rashers. It was lunch-time now and the noise had simply stopped. Two men sat on the bulwarks of a stern-trawler a hundred yards away, drinking tea and eating sandwiches. They were deep in conversation and the bulk of the trawler was between them and Robin's boat. She stepped backwards so that the pier cut her off from the water, then turned and walked back towards the town. She stopped near the public toilets. From that corner she could see Robin still contentedly playing with the engine.

In a moment he looked around. Now she saw that he was shocked. This time there was no uncertainty. He scrambled quickly over the seats as far as the bow and stretched forwards. Even from the distance she could see that he was terrified by the great gap between the boat and the pier. He shrank back at first then climbed carefully on to the little deck of the bow. He leaned over and tried to reach the rope where it trailed in the water. At length he realised that the rope itself was the same as the one that was tied at his knees to a reddened iron ring bolt. He caught it up and pulled. The boat came forwards, struck the pier and bounced back. He pulled again and held the boat tight against the steps. Now he began to scramble to get out, one leg over the side, one leg in the boat. The boat shoved off immediately and he was left hanging on, his left foot trailing in the water.

'How are you?' A man came out of the gents', zipping up his trousers. He stopped when he saw Josephine. 'You don't remember me, do you?'

She did not look at him but stared towards the child on the boat.

'Jaze, people don't be long forgetting. High and mighty now.'

'What?' she said. She looked at the man and realised that she did recognise him, but for a moment could not remember from where.

'That was desperate about the doctor's wife,' he said.

Now she was studying his features. 'You're the man from the graveyard?'

It was his turn to be puzzled. 'Graveyard? What graveyard? I knew your mother, God rest her,' he said.

'What about the doctor's wife?'

'The accident. They say she drove straight across the road. Deliberate.'

'When was that?'

But the man was staring in the same direction as her. 'That young fellow is crying,' he said. 'Of course, that solicitor, everyone knew about him. Jaze, the shock must've been desperate. And he getting engaged and all. Your one was well got they say, the one he was marrying. Rolling in it. Your one Casey hadn't a prayer. She was only the bit of fluff. Jaze, who'd marry the bit of fluff?'

Josephine shivered. 'How is your appendicitis?' she asked. He laughed. 'Gone,' he said. 'They whipped the whole lot out. So, are you working around here?'

'No,' she said abruptly. 'I'm on holiday.'

'And the little girl, what about that?'

'What little girl?'

'I never seen you at your mother's funeral.'

'No,' she said. 'I couldn't get away.'

'Jaze. What about that, hah?'

'They couldn't spare me.'

'Desperate all the same. That's my lorry over there.' He gestured in the direction of an articulated truck. Kennedy Trucking, the lorry said. 'Long distance. Good money.'

'I have to go,' she said.

'I'll be seeing you,' he said. 'I'm in The Shippe every Friday night,' he called after her. 'Drop in and I'll stand you a drink.'

Josephine rushed blindly towards the pier, feeling suddenly that the air was unbreathable, cloying and dust-filled. She found herself drawing deep breaths, heard her own coarse breathing. 'Like a horse,' she thought. 'Or a man.' She heard the breathing from her mother's room, the rapping, the sound of scrabbling and the animal moaning. The town felt suddenly claustrophobic, as though the houses had stepped closer to her, closing off all vistas. 'Destroyed,' the man called after her. 'All her face. That meningitis thing.'

When she pulled the boat in Robin was terrified. He stared up at her blankly. 'That'll teach you,' she said, catching her breath still, 'not to be so cocksure of yourself. Americans are always so cocksure of theirselves.' She pulled him roughly up the steps. 'Come on.' He trudged glumly beside her, water squelching from his left shoe. As they crossed the road she saw that the man from the graveyard was sitting in the cab of his truck sucking from a white plastic cup with a straw in it. He watched her as he sucked.

She caught Robin's hand and dragged him across the road. I should have said I was bringing my boy on a visit, she thought. I should have said I lived somewhere else. He knows. That's why he said he was in The Shippe every Friday night. She was conscious of a thread of connections where before she had seen only individual episodes, as though a group of people standing at a bus queue indifferent to each other had suddenly revealed themselves to be members of the same family: her mother's friends, her Auntie Mary's sayings, the man in the graveyard, the doctor and Jean – all seemed now to be joined in some occult series. Her past seemed burdened with unbearable significance: a significance that was barely beyond her grasp, but beyond it none the less. No coincidence that this man should be here, that he should have been at the doctor's, at the graveyard, perhaps in her mother's house once. But what did it mean? She wanted to hurry home to consult her magazines, study the questions. She chafed at the traffic that slowed her down, the people walking blindly by. The man was still there, behind the impassive forehead of his cab, watching and sucking.

She was relieved when she turned the corner. She led Robin along the rising street until they came to a small open area. Three concrete benches faced the southern sun in the arthritic shade of a pollarded poplar. On one bench an elderly man sat, twisted slightly sideways, holding a blackthorn stick between his knees, a black melanoma in the centre of his forehead like an eye.

She sat Robin on the seat furthest from the man. 'Now,' she hissed, 'did you do what I told you last night?' She looked down at the miserable face. 'You didn't did you?' Robin shook his head. 'Your body is the temple of the Holy Ghost,' she said. 'You will die in the night and go to hell and burn for ever.' Robin said nothing. 'The devil is everywhere all the time, day and night, but at night we can't see him or hear him. I want you to die in a state of grace. I don't want you to be going to hell.' She gave him a brief hug, crushing his shoulders against her. Then she released him and said, 'Well?'

'I promise,' Robin said.

'That's not good enough,' Josephine said. 'You have to do as well.'

'I'll say that prayer,' Robin said. 'The long one you told me. And I'll wash like you said.'

'And what else?'

'I won't go to the bathroom during the night in case.'

'And?'

'I won't go near the stairs.'

'You went to the bathroom before you came out?' she said. He nodded. 'Tell me what it was.' Robin's eyes flicked nervously at the traffic, the occasional passer-by. 'You know,' he said. 'Tell me exactly,' she said, stopping and folding her arms, looking down at him triumphantly. 'Describe it.' Robin turned his face towards the distant sheet of the sea where it appeared between the narrow gaps in the houses and began to describe it.

Billie Fraser was curious about the wet shoe. She left it where Josephine had placed it, under the radiator in the kitchen, stuffed with newspaper, and waited to hear the story. But Josephine did not volunteer it. Instead she chopped onions and her eyes streamed tears. In the end Billie had to ask her straight out.

'Robert won't be in for supper tonight,' she said. 'He has this lecture he has to give so he's going to grab something in that staff dining room. The food is God-awful apparently.' She fiddled with the tuning on the radio and brought out a man's voice talking about field structures in prehistoric Mayo. 'Don't you just love this?' she said. 'This place is so old. He just said 5000 BC. Fields in 5000 BC.'

'Poor Robert,' Josephine said. 'This is going to be a nice chicken casserole.' She prodded the breast and the chicken's legs wobbled apart.

'Smells excellent.' She watched Josephine at work, comfortable with her. Josephine began to hum quietly. The voice droned on, excavations, site mapping, carbon dating.

'Hey Jo, what happened to the shoe? The wet one?'

Josephine paused. 'I wasn't going to mention it,' she said. She put the knife down and turned slowly around. 'Did you talk to your friend?'

'What friend?' Dendrochronology, hunter-gatherers versus farmers.

'The psychology one?'

'No. I guess I forgot.'

'He did it again today,' Josephine said. 'He ran away when my back was turned. Only there's worse.'

'What? What worse?' Billie felt the jolt of fear, a hot knife in her bowels.

'He was down at the harbour. At the little bit of pebbly part that's there when the tide goes out. I saw him. I saw a man with him.' Billie's face blanched and she swallowed hard.

Josephine began to hum again, allowing the words to settle between them. Suddenly the radio was poetic: the great blanket of bogland that covered the Céide Fields, leaving a complex world of gardens and huts, the tidy husbandry of a six-thou-sand-year-old farm waiting to be uncovered, to be probed and exposed. Stones marking extinct boundaries. Implements lost on a harvest day so long ago. All the evidence was there.

She remembered the shapes of the pebbles on the little beach, their rounds, the reddish and brown colours, the occasional flinty white. I'm only doing this for her own good, she thought, putting her wise. She's a complete innocent when it comes to minding children. You have to be cruel to be kind. It was true. The more she understood life the more she knew that hurt and love were wound together like the strands of a steel cable, so tight that from a distance they seemed to be one substance. You had to study them hard to tell the strands apart – love and hurt – and even then it was impossible to unwind them and say this is love in this hand, and in that hand I have pain.

Then she said, 'I shouted at him and he started to run but the man sort of bumped into him, sort of shouldered him. That was how he got his foot wet. One foot went into the water. I ran around to the steps but when I got there the man was gone.'

'Oh sweet Jesus,' Billie said. She looked from left to right and back again, sudden movements, as though she were looking for a way out. Her right hand, flat on the table, was pressed down hard and the knuckles showed white and ridged.

'Now he's telling lies. He says there was no man at all. He says he never saw the man before. He has some cock-and-bull story about a boat, as if I'd let him play in a boat. It must be what the man told him to say.'

'No,' Billie said. 'No, Robin wouldn't tell lies.'

'Mrs Fraser,' Josephine said carefully, 'we all tell lies.'

She turned again to the chopping. 'I'm going to have to stop taking him out.'

'Short term,' Billie said, 'that might be a good idea.' Now she was staring at the wet shoe. 'I don't know what to say,' she said.

'And another thing,' Josephine said. 'The reason I broke it off with that boy I was seeing.'

'When was this? I didn't know you broke it off.'

'Well, there was more than one thing. But he was always asking about Robin.'

Billie Fraser stared at Josephine as though a vast field of dangers had suddenly exposed itself behind the girl's head – a minefield, a snake-filled tundra or an icy waste veined with bottomless chasms.

NINETEEN

There would be no snow but the sky threatened it anyway, a low cloud, ice in the air, a kind of luminous darkness, air made visible before their faces in the hall, ice where the dripping tap ran across the outflow and the path fretted with gleaming veins. The Frasers looked out for it. More than once Billie said that it reminded her of home. She hoped there would be a foot of snow overnight. She would like to have to shovel it off the path in the morning. The house ticked and crackled and tinkled as water was driven round the radiators, the boiler going constantly. The windows fogged. They lit a fire in the hearth and watched its cold glow for a time. In the end the day did not transcend. The Saturday traffic went on, the distant rumble of a coastal town preparing for Christmas.

Robin played with dinosaurs. He arranged them in lines

according to whether they were herbivores or carnivores. His father read the descriptions from a long chart that depicted the age of the saurians and together they separated the creatures, paying careful attention to the time period for each species. Billie read *A Vision*, tutting over Yeats's strange ideas and occasionally chuckling. Once she read out a passage about Yeats's wife and ghosts and Robin listened intently, head cocked. When he said, 'Crap!' under his breath his father looked sharply at him and said, 'I guess you shouldn't dismiss other people's ideas so out of hand, Robin. That's not the way we do it in this family. Have you ever heard Mom or me be so dismissive about each other?'

Robin gazed at the dinosaurs and said nothing.

'Come on now,' his father said. But Robin was cold, indicating by the set of his head, his whole posture, that there would be no relenting.

Billie had put down her book and she and Robert exchanged a worried glance. Then Robin brightened up and said, 'Jo had an aunt who was haunted. She had a ghost right at the top of the stairs and she had a bag of gold hidden under a step and the ghost sort of kept an eye on it. And this aunt just choked someone once, just put a plastic bag over their head and choked them. She did that because the ghost told her it was time for this someone to die, she was so old.'

'That's a good story,' Billie said. 'But it's just a story, Robin. An Irish ghost story. Like Halloween back home.'

'So, that story Mom read out, that wasn't so far out was it?' Robert said. 'You can believe Josephine, why can't you believe old W.B. Yeats? He can tell stories too.'

But Robin's coldness had returned. He nodded his head once, curtly, as though to indicate that he agreed, or that the matter was dismissed. Then he brushed four or five of the dinosaurs together and turned his back on them.

Billie got up and padded on stockinged feet to the new hi-fi they had bought a week before. Robert and Robin had spent a happy hour unpacking and assembling it and placing the speakers for maximum effect. Then they had laid down on the floor with the speakers on either side of their ears and listened for the different instruments coming in from different angles on a scratchy copy of *Abbey Road*.

She took out a new record and placed it on the turntable. She lifted the arm and brought it carefully to the beginning of the fourth track. Then, before lowering it she smiled at her husband and son. 'This is my new favourite,' she said. 'Check this out.' Carly Simon's sweet, dreamy voice, the tiny resonant notes of the piano. 'His friends are more than fond of Robin,' the speakers said. 'He doesn't need to compliment them.' Billie Fraser held the record sleeve to her chest, her hands folded across the front. Firelight glowed in her hair and she looked unexpectedly younger. When it came to the chorus she sang along: 'Robin I've never told you, but I'll be yours until we're old . . .' She turned to the room and sang it directly at the child.

'Please learn to call me in your dreams . . .' Her big, bright-toothed smile won him and he grinned up at her. 'Hey Mom, that's about me!'

When the phone rang they heard Josephine's step in the hall coming from the kitchen, the sounds muffled by the dead air. Billie and Robert looked at each other and waited, and when she passed the door a moment later they called to her and asked who it was.

'Wrong number,' Josephine said. But they knew it was Alan Wallace. They looked at each other significantly and Billie frowned.

Later, just after lunch the phone rang again and this time Billie got there first. The man on the other end asked for Josephine Strane. Billie passed the handset on silently and Josephine took it and waited until Billie left. When she hung up, Billie came out again.

'It was your friend, wasn't it?' she said softly. She folded her arms and leaned against the jamb of the living-room door.

'It was,' Josephine said. The bit of fluff. Who'd want to marry the bit of fluff.

'Don't be so cold Jo,' Billie said. 'I want to help. I count you as a friend and I'd like to be there for you when you're hurting.'

Josephine shrugged. Her face was sullen and closed, her eyes hooded.

'What'd he do, Jo? It can't be that terrible.'

Josephine made to move past her towards the kitchen then stopped. 'I don't want to talk about it,' she said.

Billie stepped back, then followed her into the kitchen. They stood looking at each other, each waiting for the other to move first. In the end Billie threw up her hands and said, 'Oh you Irish! You bottle everything up inside. You never touch anybody or hug or talk real talk. It's all platitudes about the weather and the news. No wonder this country is so neurotic. If you had one real American-style conversation in your whole lives it'd do you more good than all your religion and your literature put together. How can you *stick it?*'

Josephine's reply was cold. 'I don't know what you're talking about.'

'Look,' Billie said. 'He got fresh with you, right? What's so bad about that? Boys don't know what to do with their hands on a date. He went a bit too far. You just have to tell him the limits, that's all. Take it slowly, set your own pace. If he doesn't like it then he's not meant for you. There's plenty more fish in the sea. It's not a sin or anything. Look, kids are out there doing it all the time. It's been going on since prehistory. You do a bit, you experiment a bit, you stop, you go on. It's natural.'

'I don't know what you're talking about,' Josephine said again.

Billie sat down suddenly and put her head on her hands. She sat there a moment and then turned around and leaned out at a crazy angle to push the kitchen door closed. When it slid gently on to its latch she looked up at Josephine with an anguished look.

'Listen to me now,' she said. Her voice was strange, fainter than normal, husky. 'I'm not the best lady to be telling you what to do. I know I've got my own problems. I don't know if Robert told you that I lost my brother, oh many years ago now. Way back when I was little. I guess it had a bad effect on me. It must have had. When I had Robin I couldn't believe I was so – so blessed. It was like my little brother was back again. I know that's crazy. I know it. That's why sometimes I'm so careful. I'm an intelligent woman, I can see what I'm doing. I'm not a fool. All those plugs,' she made a tight, desperate gesture, indicating the white circles of the socket protectors. 'That's not normal. It's obsessional.' The eyes that looked out of her face were strained, the sockets darkened as though she had been crying.

'What I'm trying to tell you, you should not be like me. Don't be so careful. Live. Go out and take some chances. Be yourself. You've had a hard life but things could get better.'

Suddenly Josephine laughed. At first Billie smiled too. 'What?' she said. 'What's to laugh about?'

'You haven't a clue have you?' Josephine said. 'You haven't a clue.'

Billie straightened her shoulders. 'I guess I haven't Jo.'

'It's not myself I'm worried about,' Josephine said. 'I told you that. I don't like Alan Wallace and that's the end of it.'

'You're worrying too much,' Billie said. 'You need to lighten up on things.'

'Everything,' Josephine said with startling intensity. 'Everything means something. You have to watch out.'

'Don't you worry for Robin's sake,' Billie said. 'I've been thinking about that. It's not so bad. What you said that night, I remember it. You said he was always asking questions about Robin. I've been thinking a lot about it and there are other interpretations. In fact it's natural. He was making conversation, common ground. He knows how you love Robin and he's thinking: this is the way to her heart. That's a perfectly normal way to talk to a girl.' Josephine shook her head vigorously. 'No, no, listen to me Jo. I know what I'm talking about. He just wanted to be close to you.'

A strange pallor had come into Josephine's face, a kind of yellowed whiteness. She clasped her hands tightly together in front of her chest almost as though she were praying.

'Don't be angry at me Jo,' Billie pleaded. 'I just want to help. Sometimes I feel I know so little, and other times I feel like I'm a hundred years old by comparison with you.'

'I'm not angry,' Josephine said. 'You just don't understand.'

'What? What don't I understand? What are you thinking?'

'My mother . . .' Josephine said. She stopped suddenly, astonished at the image of her mother that had intruded, the pale half-moons of her thighs, grey flesh, a blood-stained rag. Was there someone else there? A shadow on the edge of vision, something flitting from light to darkness? A spasm passed over her face, fleeting, altering the ordinary features beyond recognition, then passing on. She turned away. Billie saw her shoulders rise and fall as though she were taking a cavernous breath. Then her voice came clear and strong: 'He tried to rape me.'

'Jesus.'

'Down at the pier.' The words tumbled out of her now. She felt the urge to pile the detail on, to elaborate, to build an edifice of meaning that would drown the memory of her mother and the rag and the shadow. 'He hit me and knocked me down. He got down on top of me and tried to stick his thing into me. He was drunk. There was blood. Shadows. I thought I would drown.' She sobbed. Dry weeping.

'Oh God no,' Billie said. 'God Jo, not that.'

Anger now, a flood of power breached her, a lust to destroy. 'And it wasn't just questions,' she spat. 'He was always asking me things. Things. Personal things about Robin.'

Billie stared at her, mesmerised.

'He wanted to know if I gave him his bath and if I went to the toilet with him. He wanted me to steal one of his underpants. He was always asking.'

Billie gasped. 'I'm just warning you,' Josephine said. 'This is a dangerous place. Get out of here before it's too late to go.'

Billie got up suddenly and rushed from the room. Josephine stared after her. 'He was a bastard,' she said to the closing door. 'A right bastard. That's why I broke it off.' My boyfriend wants me to do things: what should I do? Break it off. Advice to a girl who does not want to go too far. Never allow anyone to take over your life. Take control. Mandy, Nottingham. Give a thing, take a thing, never go to God again. One of Auntie Mary's. Meaning there was no taking back, no way out, no return. The empties going back, her mother's clear gin bottles clinking in the bag. Returns. The ghost smell of night, the sounds, the lights of cars sweeping her window. The bogeyman throwing shadows, rapping on furniture. Noise.

She was out of breath, her heart racing. She looked around the kitchen, blind to where she was. Oh Jesus, she thought, where is it coming from?

She forced herself to breathe slowly, to feel her feet on the ground, to touch the table, to see the chicken and the coffee-pot and the door. Gradually, her heart was calmed. She was able to sit down, to concentrate on preparing the food. After a time she began to hum again.

By dinner-time the threat of snow had turned to a cold globular rain that drove against the windows and ran down in wide rivers. The gutters leaked and the constant stream was like an engine running somewhere. Billie was watchful, her mood altered completely from that of the morning. Robin was sullen, complaining that he wanted to play outside, demanding to know when it was going to snow. There was no other conversation. Robert Fraser looked from his wife to his child and then to Josephine and wondered what the hell had happened.

She was aware of a dead space in her, a spreading dead zone that threatened to overrun her whole personality. When she thought about it she had a picture of a spot in the amusement park where there was a tent in the summer: no grass grew there even now, very few weeds except for the dock-roots and an occasional daisy; when it rained the soil discharged a rank moisture embellished with worm-casts; the sour smell of dead earth. She thought about it a lot. Sometimes she thought that this sterile place began the day she found Auntie Mary, as if she had been somehow infected by death. Other times she wondered if it was something she caught from her mother. She read an article in the *Readers' Digest* about a city built on the permafrost in Russia and the city itself became a symbol of it for her, not the frozen waste. Because the heat of the city had infected the permafrost with a kind of rot and the rot was spreading outwards, an ecological disaster, the beautiful frozen world slowly softening and dying.

She felt marked by it, surprised that no one else saw or sensed it. She often looked in the mirror for its outward sign. She thought of Jean suffering the inward infection that ate her brain, but marked on the outside too with the purple badge of destruction. But this dead place was invisible. There was no mark, no stain.

She found the thought painful: that no matter how she scrubbed and cleaned, no matter how careful, there would always be this corruption in her.

There were days when she felt full to the brim with warmth and love, when she held Robin's hand and felt that no harm could befall them so long as they were together. And there were times when she would push him away. Fear caught her by the throat then and she dreaded everything. Something terrible is going to happen, she told herself. She thought of every strategy to protect him. Cleanliness is next to godliness. Safety first. Look before you leap.

She scoured the magazines for a clue.

My husband has left me: what to do?

My boyfriend wants more than I can give: what to do?

I invested in a company and they have disappeared: what to do?

My daughter takes drugs: what to do?

The world was full of threats: she saw it on the television, heard it on the radio – a child disappears, an elderly woman is battered to death in her own bed, there are attempted abductions, rapes, violent assaults, a man is charged with torturing an animal, another kills a boy in a fight over his place in a fish-and-chip queue. Everywhere the world posed questions, but there *were* answers. The difficulty, she knew, was to find the right words. If you could ask the right question, the answer would be there, like a surprise in a Lucky Dip.

And she knew the question lay in the dead place, within the boundaries of that unvisitable space between her love for Robin and her fear. She felt those boundaries pulsing and expanding, invading her soul like the warming dying corruption of the permafrost. 'City of Decay,' the article said. A *Readers' Digest* Special.

'Will I tell you a story to put you to sleep?' Josephine asked. Robin nodded eagerly. 'Got another ghost story?' he asked. 'Better than that,' she said. 'I have a one about a dead man.' Robin shivered and shuffled further down under his duvet. 'Go ahead Jo,' he said.

Josephine told him about a dead man who was washed up on a cockle beach, years ago when she was still at school, his pockets full of sand and small, almost transparent crabs. She said his eyes were gone, eaten out by fish. She said his skin was withered and rucked like the skin of a rotten fish. She said that she went to see him with the other girls in her school. Someone said he was doing his wee over the side of a boat and that's how he fell out. She said his pants were open.

Robin lay with his hands folded behind his head staring into space, imagining the dead man washed in by the sea. His eyes had a dark intent look and they moved in tiny circles as though he was watching something, blinking occasional instant blinks as the story grew.

'Will I tell you what the worst thing was?'

Robin swallowed hard. 'Go ahead, tell me.'

'His thing was jelly.'

'What?'

'His thing, what do you call it?'

'His penis?' Robin said, the word taught to him as soon as he could talk, the same as any other word he needed, Billie matter-of-fact about the body, no baby-talk, no codewords, no guilt.

'Is that what you call it? It was turned to jelly. If you put your finger down on it the finger would go right in.'

Robin said yuck.

'One girl did it and she got a disease,' Josephine said. 'My Uncle Jimmy was drowned at sea in the war.' Robin turned his gaze on her, waiting patiently for the story.

'Whenever I go swimming in the sea he comes after me. The sea is haunted, did you know that?' He shook his head. 'All the sailors and people that drowned in it. Uncle Jimmy catches me by the legs and tries to drag me out. That's why I don't go swimming. He caught me once and nearly drowned me. When I was underwater I saw him. He was all mixed up with bubbles and seaweed and he had no eyes.'

'Look Robin,' she said. She took something out of her pocket and held it towards him. He leaned on his elbows and looked down at the shiny steel object in her palm.

'What *is* that?' he asked.

'A man gave it to me in a graveyard once. It's a lighter.' She flicked the head and a flame stood up out of her hand. 'He was a very bad man.' Robin stared at her. 'He had black greasy hair and hairy hands. And he died of appendicitis. Appendicitis is a stomach complaint.' She waved the flame back and forwards very slowly. 'This is his spirit,' she said.

And once her mother said, 'I don't know why you're always washing that old doll. Sure that's only an old hand-me-down doll.' Josephine cried and said that Susan was her best friend. 'Guilty conscience is all that is, that old doll,' her mother said. 'That was the only time he ever even saw you.' She remembered it now and knew that the shadow from which Susan came was her father. 'Look what the nice man brought you.' Only a shadow, a huge overcoat, a man looming against the darkness and the shining face of a doll. The only time he ever even saw her. Now he must be dead. She wanted him to be dead. To love someone and want them dead. She wished she could have loved a father. But there was no father. Only his shadow. His doll. Like a child given to her. Susan. Sister.

Some time after midnight Josephine got up and tiptoed to Robin's room. She stood above his bed a moment gazing down at him in the dull glow of his nightlight. His head was thrown back on the pillow and his mouth was open, his cheeks pinched inwards, a curious fish-like expression. His legs were doubled up almost to his stomach. His breathing was uneasy. She felt the familiar tugging at her heart. His head was a dull gold moon on the pillow, a treasure. She thought of Susan, how the sun irradiated her hair, the apple-cheeked smile and trusting blue eyes. If only Susan were alive – but then everything would be different. Susan was hers and only hers and in her deathly silence was safety and perfect love.

She heard Robin's breathing as though it were her own. She closed the door, shutting out the dim light of the landing, and was conscious of an intense feeling of intimacy, of warmth in the darkness. She felt drawn to Robin by invisible cables, and recognised the feeling as love. 'When you can't resist being with someone,' a letter had said, 'isn't that love?' And what was the answer? Yes, the need to be with a person is part of love.

Josephine bent down and shook his head roughly. 'Wake up Robin,' she hissed. 'Wake up.' He was awake immediately, eyes clicking open, then blinking, tonguing his lips and rubbing one small fist into one eye.

'What?' he asked. 'It's the middle of the night.'

'I told you,' she said. 'Keep your hands outside the blankets. Remember what I said last week about starting to rot.' There were totems, piseógs, incantations to guard the beloved: if only she could recall them. Night and day she searched for the answers. She foresaw the impending disaster, but how could she protect the child that had been entrusted to her when she believed that she herself was part of it, when the precise nature of that disaster was occult, the instruments by which it would be brought to light were unknown to her?

'Take out your hands.'

He took his second hand out quickly and joined it with the first.

'Lie on your back and join your hands like this.' She folded her hands in an X across her chest. He rolled over suddenly and copied her, looking sideways to see if she approved.

'Stay that way,' she said. 'If I see you with your hands inside again I'll tell your parents.'

'Please Jo,' he said. 'Don't tell Mom and Dad. I don't want to get rotten.'

'I'll help you Robin,' she said. My love, I will try. Love bubbling up in her, an unheralded passion. She mastered her emotion and spoke quietly, evenly, trying not to disturb him. 'It has to be a secret. I'll do everything to help you. We'll fight it together.' He nodded. She held out her left hand. 'Look. Tape.'

He sat up and gazed at the dark circle on her palm. 'What you gonna do?' he said uncertainly.

'Hold out your hands like this,' she said, showing him a flat X, palms up. He held his hands out to her and she ran three circles of tape around his wrists. Then she sealed off the tape and pushed his hands gently on to his chest. 'I'll come in early and take the tape off,' she said. 'You'll be fine.'

She closed the door quietly and saw through the landing window that there was a cold moon over the sea, the clouds broken into fragments. She saw the lighthouse beam sweep the darkness and pick out a ship almost at the edge of the visible, a grey wraith winking into existence with each sweep of the beam.

TWENTY

In the end they found him by accident. A man spinning out of season for mackerel saw something human hooked in the gleaming steel of his German Sprat and was immediately sick. The body had been damaged and fishermen said that the little fellow must have got caught in the propeller of one of the trawlers. Part of his ribcage and upper abdomen had been ripped away and a string of entrails hung out through the hole, teased out like party balloons. Part of his head was hurt too so that now the characteristic tilt seemed fixed in it, a seabird listening for ever for the weird sounds of the ocean.

The ambulance flashing wildly at the pier drew the usual crowd, but they kept the body hidden, affording glimpses only of the grey dogfish flesh, trailing fingers rucked and shrivelled from the ice-cold water. The ambulance crew went about their task in silence for the most part. A young Garda kept the crowd back.

A chip-van drew up at the top of the pier, seeing the crowd. A fat man got out and opened the huge side-door upwards, propping it up on two metal bars. His trousers hung low on his buttocks and the crease of his ass was visible where the shirt pulled up. He opened the back door humming. Soon the sickly-sweet smell of cooking chips and burgers filled the air. One or two people drifted up from the pier.

'Some poor kid,' one of them said.

'Terrible altogether,' the chip man said. He ladled out a portion of chips and put a burger on a piece of grease-proof paper.

'Make it one fifty,' he said.

A man with a dog came over. 'Small fries please,' he said. The dog pissed against the wheel of the van.

'Hi, stop that dog will you?' the chip man said. 'Ah Christ! It's too late. There's your fucking chips.'

'No call for language,' the man said. 'Tyke's his name.'

'Tell Tyke to fuck off,' the chip man said.

'No call for language,' the man said again. 'That boy fell in off a boat.'

The chip man looked at the other customer and made a small gesture with his finger to his temple indicating that he thought the man with the dog was simple.

'Messing in boats. You get people fall in and can't swim.'

He finished the last of the chips in a huge mouthful and put the paper back on the counter. 'Naughty that is, messing in boats. What's happened to his mother then? That's what I want to know. She been around today?'

The others shook their heads and winked at each other.

'I'll have a fish then,' the man said. 'Tyke likes a bit of fish.' When the chip man handed the slap of pasty batter to him he held it up and sniffed it. 'Looks good, smells good,' he said and strolled away.

Mike Smith looked at the little body and his heart quailed. Here was a child, almost the same age as his own son. His first thought was: this could be Barry. What if that bastard chucked him in the water? He saw the unmistakable signs of a beloved child – the bright clothes, the clear pale skin, decent shoes. Someone's heart would break on this.

He spoke to the boy in charge of the crowd, a young Garda stiff in his new uniform, calling him by his first name although the boy called him sir. Then he reeled away into the crowd, towards the bandstand. He stepped up on to it and leaned against the cast-iron railing, feeling his heart slowly returning to normal, his breathing slowing. This would be an accidental death, he knew. Death by misadventure as they used to say. The child playing unsupervised on the pier, perhaps not missed yet it was so early in the day. That rip in his side was an injury he got in the water, a propeller from a fishing boat it looked like. There were very few abrasions, no more than the weight of a small body sawing against the barnacles of the waterline would cause. There was a head wound, no marks on the throat. The post-mortem would confirm it all anyway.

Death, he thought, has no need of assistants. It comes unasked, does its work with very little fuss most of the time and is gone before anyone knows it has called. A kind of universal detective, slipping into people's lives, plucking certain ones out, putting them away for the duration. It takes the child as happily as the old.

Poor Barry, leaning on a support as fragile as Claire, dependent on that bastard who had never held down a job in his life. The puppeteer.

'I'm getting bloody melancholy,' he told himself and was surprised to see that a man, standing some feet away watching the crowd below on the pier, turned towards him.

'Did you speak?' the man said.

'Sorry,' Mike said. 'I was talking to myself.'

'No harm then is it?' the man said and turned back towards the pier. 'Tyke,' he called suddenly. 'Tyke?' And a small dog, smaller than a cat, darted from the ragged shrubs at the edge of the park and yapped at his feet. The man had a battered fish on a piece of coloured newspaper. He fed the dog some of the fish and continued picking at the flaking meat himself, using the same fingers that the dog had licked.

The police interviewed the Frasers and puzzled over how the boy had got out. Billie was sedated, heavy-eyed and full of tears and sighs, occasionally breaking out in a full-throated wailing that surprised and shocked the detectives. As far as they could judge, Robert Fraser was drugged too, although he was slightly more alert.

Neither of them knew anything. They had been away, one lecturing, one at a tutorial when their baby-sitter rang. She rang Robert first because she knew his office could get him. He went and found Billie. By then, according to the baby-sitter, he had been missing no more than an hour. They came straight home. They were panicked and went out searching the town. They looked in all the places Robin had been. They realised now they should have called the police. The police said nothing, knowing that a missing report that was only hours old would be treated as a joke. They could hear their sergeant: 'Bleddy yanks. Come over here and think the bleddy country is full of bleddy IRA. Be more likely to disappear in Des Moines Iowa.' Whenever the sergeant mentioned a place in America it was always Des Moines Iowa. It was a station joke. 'Who wants their bleddy kid anyway?' he would demand. 'Who'd put up with a Yankee kid whinging all the time about pizzas?' That was what he had said three years before when an American couple on holiday had reported the disappearance of their nine-year-old girl. She turned up in a boghole six months later with no clothes on but the sergeant never changed his tune.

When they had got what they could from the parents they interviewed Josephine Strane. She looked pale, diffident, unfocused. She played constantly with a button on the pocket of her jeans. She had been watching television, she said. She assumed he was in his room playing with his dinosaur collection. She held up a brown, thorny tyrannosaurus rex and looked at it. Then she sobbed. Eventually, she said, she had gone looking for him, to check up on him. He wasn't there. She searched the house and then rang Robert Fraser.

She blamed herself, she said. The boy had taken to giving her the slip recently, when they were out walking. She never expected him to leave the house, but she should have been more careful.

'There there,' the detective said, passing her a small neat packet of Posies when she began to cry. He watched the tissue flower in her hand and her face vanish into it. 'Don't blame yourself.'

'We see a lot of this,' the other detective said. 'You'd be surprised how much of it.'

'Was he inclined to go down to the harbour?'

She straightened a little, bunching the tissue and pushing it into her sleeve, pulling her legs in and crossing them at the heels. 'I used to bring him down. He liked watching the boats. The fishermen all liked him.'

'By all accounts he was a gorgeous child,' the younger detective said.

'Sometimes he used to throw stones at the water.'

They did not stay long. They pulled on their overcoats at the door and when she held it open for them they looked out into the sharp afternoon air as though looking into the future and one of them said, 'Is herself seeing a doctor?'

Josephine nodded.

'That's good anyhow. It's a terrible blow.' Josephine watched them drive away, humming quietly to herself. She felt competent, that she had things under control, that Robert and Billie were bearing up well. They had her support and need not fear that she would let them down. She would keep the house and husband their friendship until they had outlived their grief, a period that she thought of in terms of weeks. She thought of their grief as little bits of sorrow, isolated like jetsam on a beach, the leavings of another life that would be cleansed and carried away by the great tide of new things. The words of a song about death and loss came into her head – 'But it was in the early spring, when flowers bloom and robins sing, she went away, and Honey I miss you, and I'm feeling blue, and I long to be with you if only I could.'

But the police came back later, asking to see Josephine alone. They were anxious and suspicious at the same time, coming silently into the house, into the living room, sitting down without looking at her. The younger detective was the first to break the silence.

'Why didn't you tell us about this boyfriend?' he said.

Josephine gasped. 'He has nothing to do with it,' she said. 'He's away.'

They looked at each other gravely. 'Is that so?'

The other detective said, 'Since when is he gone away?'

'Before.'

'Before the little boy . . ?'

'Yes. He was gone before that.' They looked at each other again and the younger detective said, 'Still and all.'

'It happens, miss,' the other said. 'They suss out the scene and then they vanish for a bit but they come back afterwards. It's a bit of an alibi you see. We saw it before. A case we had a few years ago.'

'But he's on a course with his company,' Josephine said. 'An electronics course.'

'What company would that be?'

She gave them the name of the company and while one of them wrote it down the other said, 'It was herself remembered it. She gave us a ring at the barracks. It mightn't be important at all but we have to check it out. You should have told us.'

'You were going out with him?'

She shook her head. 'Not any more,' she said. 'We broke it off.'

'Is that so?'

'Was there a fight?'

She shook her head again. 'It was just a falling out. I didn't like him much in the end.'

'Mrs Fraser said something about questions? About the little boy?'

'That was nothing,' Josephine said. 'I should never have told her. It was just innocent questions.'

'What kind of questions?'

'Oh,' she said impatiently, 'he just wanted to know what it was like minding a small child, that's all. He was just chatting me up. The kind of thing anyone might ask.'

One of them cleared his throat. 'Mrs Fraser was inclined to think there was more in it.'

Josephine looked at the window. Darkness had fallen out of the blue and the glass was a black panel against which they were cast as a tableau. They seemed to be poised there in the slightly translucent otherworld, stiff as statues. 'Mrs Fraser has her own troubles,' Josephine said, the homely phrase more than adequate for the moment. 'She lost her brother when she was small. It affected her mind. She is,' she paused over the word, 'obsessive about things. She's inclined to suspect everybody. Look.' She stood up and went to the small bookcase that stood behind the door. She took down a book. '*Home Sweet Home*,' she read from the cover, '*Accidents at Home and in the Home Environment*. It's a book about how to stop people having accidents.'

'What about it?' they wanted to know.

'What I'm saying is she read things into everything. What she said about Alan Wallace, that was all in her head.'

'Well, we'd better get the details anyhow,' one said.

They wanted to know when and how she had met him, how often they had seen each other, what was the nature of their relationship – at which Josephine flared into brief anger. 'I didn't sleep with him, if that's what you're asking me! I have more respect for myself!' They waved their hands in help-lessness and assured her that that was not what they meant at all, not a bit of it.

'And what exactly kind of questions did he ask?'

'Oh for God's sake,' she exclaimed. 'How old was he? Was it hard to mind a little boy? Did I have to give out to him? He was only making talk.'

The detectives shrugged and looked satisfied but one of them wrote down the questions. Josephine was angry with them. She stared defiantly at the one who was writing, watching the transparent biro with the chewed top scratching laboriously across the page. Then she said, 'He drowned,' and they looked up surprised.

'That's right miss,' one of them said. 'Unless the propeller got him first. The trawler.'

'No,' she said. 'Her brother. He was drowned too. In a river.'

She remembered the drowned fisherman she saw washed up in the shallow muddy water where the best cockles were found. She recalled the strange shiver of pleasure the sight had given her. Now, in her mind's eye she regarded that shiver with curiosity, as though it belonged to someone else's past. Yes, she thought, the drowned man had looked up at her with empty sockets and although she had seen him, he could never look at her. She had felt some kind of power. Suddenly, sharply, she recalled the smell of rot and sea. It was the smell of the harbour where torn fish and broken crab-shells littered the weed. Salt. Flesh. Water.

Afterwards, in school, there was one girl who joked about him, coarsening his death. Josephine remembered seeing a man relieving himself by the side of the road. She did not think of the man pissing when she thought about his death. Instead she imagined him being washed away in a heroic struggle with the sea. Drowning was not a bad death. So Auntie Mary said. She said it was serene, not like some other ways.

'They do get careless,' one of the detectives said. 'These fellows.'

'Who?'

'You know. People who do kids. They usually do a few. Then they get careless.' He seemed to find the repetition consoling, as though the probability of a successful prosecution was increased with each incantation.

'He was only making talk.'

'Just the same, we'd want to check it out.'

'We'd want to follow up all avenues of enquiry,' the other said.

'In case. But that's our experience. They keep at it until they make a mistake.'

The younger of the two detectives phoned the following day. They had interviewed Alan Wallace, or at least the Dublin lads had interviewed him. He was up there studying electronics, on a company course. They didn't think he could have got down from Dublin to do anything in the timescale they had. They were checking with his teachers but they guessed his alibi would stand up. He said he was in class all the time. The hotel he was staying in would confirm he was in before ten. The Dublin lads were inclined to believe him.

It looked like an accident, a tragic accident. No foul play suspected.

Later they called at the house and spoke to the Frasers alone. They parked their car on the road outside and Josephine heard the crackle of a radio through the half-open window.

They said how sorry they were, that this kind of thing happens and there was nothing anyone could do to bring him back and blaming themselves was wrong too. They said they came across all kinds of things in their line of work and people often thought the worst. That someone had taken the child and done things, but at least in this case they were sure that it was only the drowning. The post-mortem would confirm it they felt sure. It was a tragedy, pure and simple, a desperate human tragedy. They wanted to offer Mrs and Mr Fraser the sympathy of the entire barracks and all the force. They stood up and shook hands and went away gravely but with a sense of having achieved something, of having behaved correctly. As the car pulled away one of them was already talking into the radio microphone.

When they left, Robert went out abruptly, dragging a coat from the hall-stand, slamming the door. For all his numbers and his secret signs and his books, Josephine thought, he doesn't understand a bit of what is happening to him now. She smiled at the thought of it. She, Josephine Strane, knew and understood all of it. Professor Robert Fraser hadn't a clue. She thought of the names of his books: *Man And His Symbols, The Lure of Large Primes*. She knew them by heart, had taken possession of them. She knew their titles and the authors and who had published them, almost every book he owned. Sometimes she recited them like a poem, rearranging them so that the titles fitted. Sometimes the titles came out as a song, except there was only a rambling air to it, not real music except the names themselves: Marin Mersenne, Pierre Fermat.

Billie came to the kitchen door and stared at Josephine.

'They say it was an accident,' she said.

'I think it was,' Josephine said. René Descartes. Rowan Hamilton.

'He sneaked out and fell in the water?'

'Yes.' The Cartesian Plane. The Prime Number Theorem.

'Not me. I don't buy it.'

Josephine remained silent.

'He wouldn't do that. He was a good boy. A good boy.'

'He was,' Josephine said. Robert understood all this, the magic of numbers, the obscure letters and symbols. Like the field structures that someone discovered buried under bogland in the west of Ireland, he knew the shapes that lay beneath the surface, could graph the structures. He knew their real beauty and she, Josephine Strane, would never grasp it, never know more than the simple surface of things, the gloss, the sheen, the blush. Never delve below. Never get beyond the poetry of the name. But in this case, in just this one case, where his life was crumbling, everything losing its shape – in this case, she knew everything. She had the map, the graph, the equation. She held all the power. She could put the pieces together again, reshape his existence, his family. And perhaps this power would lead her onwards, opening doors, books, worlds. She smiled her tight little smile.

Billie advanced two paces and then stopped. Josephine saw that her face was a mixture of aggression and despair. Her eyes were puffed and surrounded by crescent moons. Her skin was moon-grey, her hair was a dull tarry colour, flattened on to her scalp, one lick falling across her forehead looked wet as if she were sweating. 'You said he wasn't. You said he was bold.'

'That was only small things. He was a lovely boy really.' She could not concentrate on what Billie Fraser was saying. Here was a truth about herself, something to be grasped that was just out of reach. She wanted peace to think it through, not Billie's carping questions. She was suddenly acutely aware of herself in relation to Robert's knowledge. She saw her whole life in stark contrast with it: the ignorance and blindness of her education; the mysteries of her childhood; her aunt and her mother. These were things that she had not seen in isolation before. Now they stood out as problems. If she could understand these things, peel off the blanket of confusion, she thought perhaps she could build on them. She was moved by a tremendous excitement, felt on the verge of discovery.

'You poisoned him.'

Josephine was shocked. 'Mrs Fraser! Sure, he drowned!'

'His mind. You twisted it all.'

Josephine began to shake, a tremble beginning in her right leg and extending through her body. She noticed the shake as though it belonged to someone else. She made an effort to control it, managing to make her hands sit still in front of her. She looked at them with interest, the short fingers, the stubby knuckles, not pale thin hands like Billie's, more the colour and texture of uncooked pastry.

'You changed him. He was a beautiful boy, our little Robin. You changed him.' Tears streamed down Billie Fraser's face. She clutched and unclutched the pockets of her cardigan. 'Back in the States he was always happy. We made sure of that. What did we do wrong? We should never have come over here, never.

I shouldn't have left him, just handed him over like that. I should've been at home.'

Josephine looked at her and relaxed. It was no longer an effort to control the shaking. The tremors were dying out like ripples from a splash weakening as they left the centre. 'Get a grip on yourself Mrs Fraser,' she said. 'There's no use crying over spilt milk.' That was one of Auntie Mary's. No use crying over spilt milk.

'What did you say? What did you say?' She shook her head as though clearing some impediment, shaking her head clear of whatever was interfering with her hearing. 'I'm not hearing this!'

'You'll be all right. You'll get over it.'

Billie's eyes opened clear all of a sudden. 'Who are you?' she asked. 'I know nothing about you. I gave my baby to you and what do I know?'

'I'm just the child-minder,' Josephine said. 'I mind children.'

'You didn't mind Robin,' Billie said.

'He did it himself Mrs Fraser,' Josephine said. 'Don't go blaming me. He sneaked out the way the guards said and he fell into the water and drowned. He did it himself. Not me.'

'Get out!' she yelled. 'Get out of our house. Don't ever come back again. Get out now!' She advanced on her, fingers hooked, teeth bared. Josephine picked up the chopping knife she had been using and held it before her uncertainly. Billie Fraser looked at the knife and turned on her heel. As she went through the kitchen door she said, 'Leave before Robert gets back.'

TWENTY ONE

The funeral passed slowly along the waterfront and paused at the foot of the hill that led up to the house. Then it moved on, the black hearse with the white coffin leading. She counted eleven cars following. Not much of a turn-out. Eaten bread is soon forgotten, that was one of Auntie Mary's. She wondered how many cars were at her mother's funeral. One or two – the gleaming descendants of old Escorts and Anglias parked away from the light on November evenings. But these cars contained people from the university, one or two neighbours, the man who owned the estate agent's. She saw their faces and recognised their indifference. Funerals were mostly business for them.

She stayed in the shadow of the bandstand until the last car disappeared on the long left-hand curve that led out to the

Protestant graveyard. The Frasers didn't go to church there: in fact, she remembered Robert Fraser saying they didn't believe in God, but Church of Ireland was the nearest thing to the faith they were brought up in. It was hypocrisy, she knew, but she found she could not despise it. She was proud of that, conscious that it involved a certain magnanimity on her part. People cling to things in their grief, she thought. She had watched the grey-suited minister go into the house with a bundle of papers under his arm. He had red and blue biros in his top pocket. A pale-faced woman waited behind in the black Rover. Mrs Minister. She read a magazine while she waited. Josephine walked slowly past and saw that it was a three months old *Woman's Weekly* featuring Princess Grace of Monaco, full of photographs of that perfect face, the fairy-tale wedding. She had a copy herself. It was in her collection upstairs in the Frasers' house.

When the minister came out Josephine knew by the way he walked that everything had been arranged. In Christian charity the Church of Ireland would bury little Robin among their substantial stones, his name on a square of limestone or marble among the Simmondses, the Eggeshawes, the Smiths, the Ffrenchs, the Beardsleys. When the car had moved a hundred yards from the house, Josephine saw Mrs Minister break into animated conversation, the funeral-going face dissolved in coquettish smiles and flashing eyes. Not such a dry stick then.

When the last car was gone she went down to the pier and sat on the steps looking out on the boat. The water was glassy and still, purpled by diesel as always. The boat sat at the end of its rope like a toy.

A thin man in an Aran cardigan came along the pier towed by a tiny white dog on a long chain. He stopped near the steps while the dog pissed against a bollard. He nodded to Josephine.

'What you done with him then?' he asked. His accent was difficult to pin down, a hint of Englishness. Josephine ignored the question. The man cleared his throat and said again, 'What you done with him then?'

He came forwards, head jutting, eyes bright with anger.

'Ask a civil question,' he said, 'expect a civil answer.'

'I don't know what you're talking about,' Josephine said.

'Your boy,' the man said. 'Your boy, what you done with him?'

'I don't know you,' Josephine said, rising to go. But he barred her way so that she was forced to take a single step down, conscious of a litter of broken shell under her feet, of the water behind her, the boat, the hulks of the trawlers straining their mooring warps.

'I know you though, don't I,' he said. 'I seen you every time. Down here with your boy. Messing about in that boat. And down there,' a nod of the head towards the apron of pebbles at the high end of the harbour. 'Messing about throwing stones in the water.'

'I never saw you before,' she said. He seemed to be un-naturally tall, rising miles high above her. Looking down.

'Nice kid,' he said. Suddenly he appeared to relax. His left hand slipped deftly through the eye of the leash and both hands went to the pockets of his Aran cardigan. They dragged the cardigan down so that he looked even more elongated, more unnatural, a caricature. Josephine noticed that a dandruff of potato crisp had collected in the fabric of his shirt about his waist. His skin was waxy. It reminded Josephine of something, the waxy skin and the strange pallor and the appearance his skin had of being wrapped tightly in cellophane. Then she saw that there was a black-blue mole like a crushed fly on his upper lip and she remembered her Auntie Mary and knew that this was the memory that she was trying to grasp. She smiled at the thought: Auntie Mary lying on the bed in the soft swinging light of the morning and the ash-trees and the bluebottle moving in and out of her mouth like a child darting in and out of a hiding place.

'Yes,' she said. 'Very nice.'

'Not all nice these days,' the elongated man said. 'Nasty sometimes. They throw stones at Tyke.' He nodded his head at the dog. 'Tyke,' he said, by way of introduction.

'Nice dog,' Josephine said.

'Mongrels are the most intelligent,' the man said. 'I seen him messing about on that boat. That's dangerous, that boat is. Naughty.'

Naughty. That word. She knew that she was safe when she heard it, that he was half imbecile. She smiled again, suddenly conscious of the warmth of the day, of the feeling of closure that the passing of the funeral had brought, a sense of new beginnings growing out of old dead things.

'That's right,' he said. 'Boats are dangerous. What you done with him then.'

'His father is taking him to the pictures,' she said. She laughed and clapped her hands suddenly together at the idea. The man smiled warily back. 'For a treat.'

'That's nice,' the man said. 'A treat. What age are you?'

'Nineteen,' Josephine said.

'You're quite young, quite young.'

'I'm not really,' she said. 'He's three. I had him when I was sixteen.' The man whistled. 'Sixteen.'

'His father and I, we just knew we were made for each other. We couldn't wait. Of course, my parents had an awful fit, but in the end they agreed. He's a doctor, my husband. He knows all about that kind of thing. He said sixteen wasn't too young.'

'That's nice, a doctor,' the man said.

'So we got married and had the baby.'

'Nice kid.'

'Oh beautiful. Did you notice his eyes. They're the same blue as the sky.'

'That's what I told them, blue eyes,' the man said.

'And he liked boats. He always liked to come down here and play on the boats.'

'Dangerous,' the man said. 'Messing. You get people fall in

and can't swim.' He made a gurgling sound and raised one hand above his head, waving it frantically. Then he lowered the hand and looked down at it. 'Messing in boats,' he said.

'And throw stones at the water. He's gone to see the pictures now with his daddy, and I'm going home in a minute to cook something nice for the two of them, one of their favourites.'

'That's nice, cook something nice.' She nodded eagerly and he nodded back, face a soft cushion of smiles. She explained to him that she had been teaching herself to cook, that she had magazines with thousands of recipes, that she could cook boeuf bourguignon and pot-au-feu and chicken cacciatore. 'Very nice, chicken,' the man said. She told him that she believed in improving herself, developing new skills, and she described her method to him and how taking it out of the casserole half an hour before the end and just crisping the skin on an open dish made the whole thing unique, her special signature.

'I seen you up the town,' he said, smiling and winking. 'You were playing hide.'

Josephine shivered. 'One of our games. The bogeyman.'

'That's what I said. Tyke can't swim. I don't never let him near the water. Dangerous.'

'The dog?'

'He's my dog.'

'Nice dog.'

'Thank you very much.'

'I have to go.' She looked along the pier and saw one of the fishermen making his way towards them. He was carrying something heavy that dragged him down on one side. It could have been an outboard motor in a plastic fertiliser bag, an awkward bundle, or out-of-season salmon netted in the deep fast-running water off a headland.

'It's been a pleasure,' the man said. He did not step aside, so that Josephine was obliged to slip by the bollard, her feet skirting the edge of the pier, the rounded stones. She stepped over the blackening piss-stain that had run out of the dog, run out like a river delta through the unevenness of the pier.

'He couldn't swim could he?' the man said. 'That day. You should have thrown the life-ring. That's what I say. Look,' he pointed along the quay at the red and white ring in its gleaming white frame. 'Life-ring see.'

Now she could place the accent. She had heard it before. One of those men who called on her mother had it, someone who had worked in England. She remembered that he smelled of some kind of hair oil. 'How's your Mum then,' he would say. 'Is she about? Come on dear,' he would call as her mother delayed over the details of her face, 'you're not going to the Pally you know.'

She saw the hearse pass back along the waterfront, gliding on silent wheels, empty now, no white coffin, no flowers, bereft. 'I never saw you,' she said. The fisherman passed, glancing at her. Did he recognise her? She seemed to detect pity in his look.

'I seen you all right,' he said. 'Hiding, see? Up the gents' toilet.'

She watched the fisherman going up towards a battered old Opel Kadett estate. He opened the hatchback and heaved the fertiliser bag in. Then he stopped and leaned on the edge of the roof and gazed down at the pier. He could have been watching her, or he could have been watching something else. She spoke quietly, with studied evenness. 'What did you see?'

The man took his hands from the Aran cardigan and transferred the leash from the left hand to the right. With the left hand he wiped his nose on his sleeve and looked down at the watery grey mark it left. 'Nice kid,' he said. 'That's what I said.'

'What did you see?'

'Not much, did I? Fog. I said to myself boats out there today, they'll get lost. Foghorn going all day.' He made a moaning sound. 'Foghorn on the lighthouse.'

'It was a foggy day all right.'

'Oh yes, fog.'

She remembered that Robin said the fog reminded him of sheep, all woolly and stuff. She thought of the drifts of fog as huddled sheep in corners. She remembered saying that fog was dangerous, that you could get lost in it, and Robin laughed, thinking of hide and seek.

'Cold too, fog is.'

'Yes,' she said. 'Fog is very cold.'

'That's what I said. Cold down the harbour in fog. I said, boys should wear pullovers in the cold. Too cold to go in the water, I said. Dangerous.'

'Who did you say it to?'

'Up the town,' he said. 'I got Tyke his Pedigree Chum. He likes Chunky Beef.' The dog lay down suddenly, its tiny tongue a lolling obscene medal, its forepaws stretched out in front, tiny claws of ivory the texture of translucent slugs. 'Your boyfriend,' he said and stopped suddenly, embarrassed.

'What about my boyfriend?'

'Naughty naughty,' the man said, waving a finger on the hand that had the leash looped on it. He blushed and stared at the dog. His eyebrows arched downwards, a line of tangled wire disintegrating into fluff at the edges.

'You were spying!'

'No no,' he said. 'No I never. You were out in the open. Plain as the nose on your face it was.' She remembered how she had splayed herself, his hand forced into the hard fabric of her denims. She remembered her sounds, movements. 'Show me your knickers,' Auntie Mary had said. I know what she was looking for. She thought it was me too. Common filth. And the Frasers? What did they think of her? How much did they know? How much could a man know who knows the numbers of things and the secret signs?

'Would you like to go for a walk?' she said, a knot of fear in her stomach.

'Walk the dog,' the man said. 'Tyke.'

'That's right,' Josephine said. 'You could show me where you were hiding.'

Suddenly the man was agitated. He swayed from one leg to the other and twitched the leash, jerking the dog sharply backwards. He shook his head. 'Not the gents',' he said.

'It's all right,' she said. 'I'll be there.'

'Not the gents',' he said again. 'Got to go home haven't I. People be asking questions. Got to get back.'

'I like you,' she said. She turned her warmest smile on him.

'No,' he said. 'You slept up the bandstand last night. That's what I said.'

He began to move away from her.

'Wouldn't you like to do something?' she said. 'Up the gents'? Come on. You like to watch. I'll let you watch.'

He shook his head and began to walk rapidly, dragging the reluctant dog. Josephine ran to catch up but when he heard her steps he began to run too, a heavy lumbering pace, half skipping half running, and Josephine knew she couldn't follow. The fisherman had slammed the boot and was sitting in the driver's seat with one leg in and one leg out. He watched the man and the dog go past and then stared down at Josephine. She stopped in the middle of the pier and made a deliberate effort to laugh. Then, unexpectedly, laughter came easily, bubbling up from inside, a strange erotic rush. She stood watching the man lolloping along and the weird sound flooded out of her and the weird spasms convulsed her stomach and her diaphragm, and her face twisted itself out of control.

In the end the seizure passed. The man in the Aran cardigan was gone. The fisherman still stared at her through the salt-speckled windscreen. She stared back at him until he closed the door and started the engine. The Opel pulled slowly round in a tight circle, reversed back almost to the edge of the pier and then accelerated up the slope in a cloud of blue smoke.

She watched him leave.

The funeral was over now. One more night and it would be safe to go back. Just one more night in the freezing half-shelter of the bandstand, the noisy drunks and courting couples keeping her awake long into the small hours, the freezing cold in the morning. Not a day too soon, she thought. The sky was low and there was every sign of bad weather. She had heard someone say that there was a hurricane coming tomorrow, that today was the calm before the storm. She imagined the hurricane leaving the coast of Florida, where it had caused flooding and torn roofs off houses, and swinging east across the broad Atlantic, whipping up the sea into a fury and driving long waves before it to fall on this coast. The pictures she saw on the display television in Bolster's Electrical Appliances window did not give any idea of the power, just a white curl on the blank of the ocean, a figure a child would draw, or something from Robert Fraser's books. But the film from Florida showed roofs blowing off and trees bending double. It would be no fun in the bandstand on a night like that. She had seen a storm here before, the waves breaking against the distant lighthouse on its little island, exploding above the breakwater, screaming in the poles and the rigging of the trawlers. She had seen the wrack of land-life pulled down from the crumbling cliffs, the bedsteads, barrels, fence-posts, old cookers, bottles: the cliffs themselves, their faces scoured and renewed every winter. She thought of the sea as the great cleansing department rooting out the detritus of the world's edge, paring lives down to the barest bone, taking up the waste and the disposable. She did not wish to be at the edge when the storm launched itself. She shivered at the thought of the onslaught, what it would be like to huddle in the bandstand with the great jaws tearing at the world.

She would return to the Frasers tomorrow and show them that she could be different, that she could forgive and forget. No hard feelings, she would say. She had seen something like that in *Woman's Own* or *Woman's Realm* or one of the other magazines in her collection. 'Go back and confront your pain,' had been the advice. 'Show them that you share it and together you can build a new life.' She remembered that because it was signed 'Distraught Josephine'. Her own name. She would go to the post office and withdraw some of her money and buy them all their favourite things. She would cook a perfect meal, one of the recipes from *Good Housekeeping*. She would buy wine and garlic bread and it would be a romantic meal, just the three of them. It would help them to forget Robin.

She would have to go back because she had left things: her magazines, her clothes. Above all there was Susan. In the ideal home and garden, the owner had a collection of Victorian dolls. All the gleaming faces. Susan's dress needed repair. There was a tear along the hem. Clumsy me. Dressing after her bath, a tear, an easy thing to do. Susan never complained. Although Josephine bathed her daily, she was never dirty. She looked at her with trusting eyes and slept when she was told. And there, under the bed, the store of wisdom, the questions and the answers, the cool interiors of other people's homes, the glazed beauty of *Homes & Gardens.*

And anyway she would need her reference if she were to move on.

And then she thought of Robin perched on the side of the boat, holding on tight because of the rocking motion, and she heard his cries like the trilling of a bird, remote and incomprehensible, a kind of animal code. She wondered what he looked like in the coffin, his hands crossing the X high up on his chest, and whether they had cleaned up the rip in his side that the propeller had made.

TWENTY TWO

'Mike?'

He sighed. 'Hang on a sec,' he said. He put the receiver down and pressed the off button on the remote control. The television screen hissed and collapsed inwards to a point of vivid light, the bad news going out in a blaze of glory. 'OK,' he said wearily. 'What is it this time Claire?'

'Fuck you,' she said.

'Is that what you rang me up for? I haven't the time to listen to more of that. I'm expecting a call.' Just before leaving the station he had sent two lads around to the hospital to try to get a statement. They phoned back an hour later to say that the man was in the psychiatric wing now and should they still try. He could hear their nervousness, hoping he would say no don't bother if he's a loony, you'll get nothing, go home. But it was a strange case and he wanted to find out. He had sent them onwards. They should be checking in any minute. The man had been found locked in the gents' toilet on the waterfront. Someone had bought a brand-new padlock to do the job. People had been attracted to the toilets, which had not been locked in years, by the sound of wailing. They found that the man's dog had been jammed into the bars of the gate with enough force to crush the dog's skull on either side. He had looked at it himself for once, although he hardly ever seemed to get out of the office these days, curious about a kind of crime that didn't usually happen in the seaside town. There were thin trails of blood on the dog's flanks and the rust had been scratched away where its hind legs had scrabbled in its death-throes. The man was completely incoherent, having spent the night hunkered on the furthest toilet seat, terrified to come out. Kids it would be. Bastards, some of these kids were these days. What kind of people would they grow up to be?

There was a short pause. 'Look. Mike,' she said. He knew by the hesitation that things were different. He wondered if the puppeteer had walked out on her, or brought another woman home, or got stoned out of his head. Or maybe he was in gaol.

'What?'

He heard her exasperated gasp, as if she had been holding her breath. 'Shit. It's not working out, is it?'

'What?'

'This thing. Look, he doesn't get on with Barry.' Mike's heart leaped. 'He likes him and all that, and he likes kids, but there's a personality clash. You know what I mean? He needs time to get used to him.'

'He's only had a few months.' He couldn't resist that, but she took it at face value. Claire's lover was the kind of man who didn't relate well to anybody, much less a child. Perhaps he related to Claire?

'Exactly. He needs more time.' She paused. 'So we're going away. We're going to England. To start a new life. London.'

'What about Barry?' The question was spat out, an inter-rogator's habit, get to the point.

'That's what I'm telling you,' she said.

'What are you telling me?'

'You can have him back.' *You can have him back.* A toy, a borrowed garden tool, a paperback. You can have it back. A bully backing down and returning the purloined treasure.

'Bitch.'

'Mike, please. Don't be like that. We can't take him.' She had misunderstood his anger. 'We'll be squatting maybe first, or anyway staying with friends. It won't be easy until we can set up our business.'

'What business? Puppets?'

'Puppets and pottery. We're going into the toy business. Quality toys. Craft toys.'

'Which no kid wants to play with.'

'That's your point of view. There are plenty of people who

want good quality things. They're tired of plastic. Especially in London.'

'They'll get very tired of stupid bloody puppets that don't work!'

They fought it out for a few minutes until the full truth dawned on him: Barry was coming back. Once he had him she would never again get her hands on him. She was leaving the jurisdiction. She was proposing to live in a squat. He made a mental note to get Jim Greene of the Met to do a check on her. Jim would do it for him. With a little bit of luck she would be picked up for possession or drunk and disorderly. Anyway, he had applied for a transfer and by coincidence it had come through together with promotion to inspector. The envelope was on top of the television. He had taken no satisfaction in it when he opened it this morning, but now suddenly, it was miraculous, the first turn of good luck he had had since Barry was born and Claire had taken to calling him 'cop'.

'Look, Claire,' he said, deliberately injecting reason, affection even, into his voice. 'Look, let's not fight now. We're talking about our baby. Our Barry.'

Suddenly she began to cry. He could hear her muffled gurgling and sniffing. Don't hang up, he thought. Please Claire, don't hang up.

'Don't cry, Claire,' he said, wheedling now. 'We did our best. We were never going to work out. We're opposites. They say opposites attract but it isn't true. Or if they do they don't get on anyway.' He was making it up, dredging the pseudo-psychology rubbish from the back of his mind, stuff he had seen on soap operas and films. 'We were never meant for each other.' He knew she would fall for that one. She would see it in their stars, the doomed couple, Romeo and Juliet.

'Too true,' she said. 'You're absolutely right Mike. It isn't our fault. We were never meant for each other.'

And that's it, he thought. Absolution. You were unfaithful to your husband, you walked out on him, you used your child to get at him, but it is written in the stars so you're not guilty. Not guilty by reason of Destiny.

'Barry,' he said. 'What happens next?'

'We're going on the boat. Tomorrow.' He gasped.

'Tomorrow. The boat? That's two o'clock.' He had a few of the lads watching the boat for the past two weeks on the strength of a tip-off from British Customs and Excise. A matter of a van-load of dope. A red Hiace van, Irish reg. He was familiar with the schedule.

'That's it.'

'It's very sudden.'

'Yeah, well, we don't hang around. When we make our mind up we go for it.'

He had a meeting at nine thirty. 'I can't pick him up until midday.'

'That's OK. We'll drop him over tonight.'

'You can't wait to get rid of him, can you?' he said, finally unable to control his contempt.

'Yeah, well, like I said. We go for it.'

'So. What are you doing tonight? Apart from the obvious. A bit of a farewell party.'

'A few friends.'

'Well don't get caught with anything that might detain you in this country.'

'Bastard fascist. You'd love that.'

The Toyota was noisier than ever. Mike thought with relish that they would never get as far as London. The car would be held at Swansea until they got a silencer for it, and he suspected they didn't have the money for that.

Claire got out with two small bags and brought them up the path. He was surprised that Barry's things were so slight. Barry himself was asleep on the back seat, the crop-eared teddy bear clutched tightly to his chest.

'Come in,' he said. He nodded his head at the car. 'Does he want to come in? The puppeteer?' She shook her head.

They sat in the living room in front of the dead grey face of the television and looked at each other.

'Well, Mike,' she said.

'This is it so,' he said.

'We had some good times.'

Oh Jesus no, he thought. What re-run of what 1950s weepy

was she playing out now. There had been very few good times, none that sprang immediately to mind, certainly none in the last four years.

'Claire I don't want to go over it now,' he said. 'I'm not nostalgic about it. You walked out on me, but the whole shooting match was over long before that. Like I said on the phone, we should never have married.'

'You're a cold bastard.'

'I suppose I am.'

'The trouble with you is that inside there somewhere, buried under the cop, is a real human being. You're just out of touch, that's all. If you could get back in touch with your real self you'd be much happier and more fulfilled.'

'I've been listening to that crap from you for years now,' he said. 'You're not exactly a good advert for it.'

'That's below the belt.'

He made an open-handed gesture, a kind of giving up. 'You'll have to send me a forwarding address.'

She flared suddenly. 'Like frigging hell I will. When I want you I'll get in touch with you. I know your cop ways. You just want to keep an eye on me. You want to get your frigging pals in London to get the shit on me. Well, no way José. Don't call us, we'll call you.'

He shrugged. 'Have it your own way. I was just thinking that there might be things I'd need to pass on to you.'

'No thanks.'

'OK.'

'I'll be off so. He had his dinner. He mightn't even wake up when I move him. What are you going to do about minding him?'

'I saw an ad in Buckley's, the newsagents. A child-minder, very experienced it says. Josephine something. Excellent references, it said.'

'That's all right so.'

'Don't worry about him.' His voice was suddenly thick, remnants of the desire that had drawn him to her years before clogging his vocal chords, moistening his eyes. She looked at him. 'Don't get weepy on me Mike.'

'I won't,' he said.

'Take care of yourself.'

'I will. You too.'

'Cheerio so.' She leaned forwards and pecked him suddenly on the cheek.

She lifted Barry out and passed the bundle, still sleeping, to him. Mike inhaled the peculiar vegetable-and-herbal-tea smell that the child gave off. That's the last of that, he thought. Rashers and sausages for breakfast for you my boy.

The puppeteer said, 'Best of luck Mike,' as though it were Mike who was setting out on a journey. He did not look round as Barry was carried up the path. Claire lingered a moment at the passenger door. She lifted her hand and made a slight waving motion. With what he could spare of his left hand he waved back, then she got into the car.

The huge rumbling startled him, filling the space between the houses with ominous echoes. He looked up as they drove away and noticed that the lights of the town were glowing red on the lowering clouds. He remembered that the weather forecast had issued a severe weather alert for tomorrow, some half-spent hurricane coming to tear the country apart. It would be a busy day: powerlines would fall on people; cars would be lifted by the wind and thrown at each other on dangerous bends; there would be coastal rescues, elderly people to be taken from homes violated by creeping water; walls would collapse and block traffic. The sea would suck and surge and throw up its secret vices, and woodlands and heaths and boglands would give evidence of their furtive encounters. Bodies would come to light in the wind's dredging, and sins would be disclosed, and each new thing would be a disaster in someone's life. He had seen it all before, the random violence that Nature revelled in – death, injury, the destruction of treasured possessions, each suffering household the victim of a tiny element in the gross chaos that was a storm. As though someone had pulled the pin of a hand-grenade and tossed it into the middle of a family meal, casually, no personal malice intended, a small, infinitely destructive piece of vandalism.

But tonight he cradled Barry in his arms: there would be no explosion in his house, his roof was dry, his walls were sound. He had his child and the two of them would face the storm with equanimity. He felt indestructible, full of confidence in the future. First thing in the morning he would phone about the ad, the child-minder. First thing, before the wind had a chance to rattle the telephone lines and cut him off. Then he would phone the station and reschedule the meeting. He had a good feeling about the ad.

As he stood there his mood was shattered by the sound of the telephone ringing. It would be the two lads calling from the asylum. He remembered the tiny dog's skull jammed between the rusty bars, the trickle of blood. The skull had been hammered in place by a stone. Now he remembered another detail. Black electrical tape held the dog's body against the bars and the front paws had been taped together.

He stuck his shoulder to the door and slammed it in a sudden rage against the sullen threatening night and Barry's body stretched and his eyes opened, big blue eyes confused to wake where he hadn't fallen asleep, still half-dreaming. Mike looked down at his son's frail face. 'Hello Barry,' he said. 'It's Dad. You're safe now.'

'Mike? There's something funny about all this.' He could hear the hollowness of a hospital behind the voice, an echo-chamber of closing doors and moving feet. Barry was dozing on the couch. He would have to be moved to bed. Better put him in mine, he thought. For tonight anyway. The child had his thumb in the side of his mouth, a tiny rivulet of spittle leaking below his fist.

'Tell me.'

'No problem getting him to talk, it's getting him to stop is the problem. They sedated him but they'd want to double the dose in the opinion of yours truly. Anyway you know the American kid? The kid that drowned? He says he saw it. He says it was the mother.'

'Jesus.' He considered it for a second, recalling with an effort the files that had landed on his desk. 'No, that was checked out. Who was on it? Anyway the mother was at a lecture or something. It checked out.'

'But look, listen to this. Listen, he says she was nineteen. The mother. He says she told him herself.'

'It doesn't add up.'

'We're coming over. You better see our notes.'

He could hear the excitement. He said, 'Don't ring the bell. I'll let you in. I have Barry back. He's worn out. He'll be in bed asleep.'

A short silence, then – 'Well that's good news anyway.' Another short silence. 'Isn't it?'

'Mathematics and creativity alfred adler the four colour problem haken appel.' She sings her rambling song, and as she sings she flicks the head of the lighter and the flame jumps into existence and dies again, on and off, on and off. It casts no light against the blockade of the fog. 'A handbook of mathematical logic the way things are by p.w. bridgemen,' she sings. The fog fills the seaward side with a single grey wall. There is nothing there but the low moaning of the foghorn, the invisible light whirling in emptiness, the sucking and spitting of the sea. Uncle Jimmy never came back. I can swim now, she thinks. No ghost will pull my legs down. Uncle Jimmy floating in the wreck of his minesweeper somewhere off Spitzbergen, that was what her mother said.

Off Spitzbergen. Once she had looked it up in her school atlas. It was a tiny speck on the frozen top of the world. Afterwards she tried to think of Uncle Jimmy petrified in the act of returning, but always the image melted and he was suddenly freed from the purity of ice to pursue her.

Drowning is not the worst way.

The truth is he would be trapped inside the ship because he worked down there, somewhere low in the belly where the engines were. She thought of the room where he was as narrow and low-ceilinged because his ship was only a small one, the narrow passageways alive with fine dark fronds and patient fishes. Auntie Mary said his hands always smelled of grease and his skin was marked with veins of black. But where were his eyes? The sea flowed in and out of the sockets of his skull and small fish made their home there, haunting the place where his memories had been.

Let the dead bury the dead.

Robin's hands are pale, the colourless white of the fog. He snatches at the edge of the boat when she twists it, his hands clutching at the timber of the edge and slipping off. The splash he makes is swallowed up by the fog. There are other splashes for a time, and his voice, full of water, bubbling and spitting, saying Jo Jo Jo.

Pick me up on your way down, she thinks then, the notes and words curling and swimming in her head, joyful, carolling. You may be their pride and joy but they'll find another toy and they'll take away your crown, pick me up on your way down.

'Charlie Walker,' she tells Robin and the closed silent harbour.

She feels something coming to life in her, as if the dead space she has felt for many weeks has been sent rain and sun and now, burgeoning and joyful, green life springs from it. Susan will notice, she thinks. She sees everything. Her eyes are like Robin's, the same colour, the same open trust as when she met him first, unchanged, untarnished. A renewal of vows. Many couples find their relationship gets that extra something after they have renewed their vows in a special ceremony. 'It's just like when we first met,' says Mrs Haskett from Nuneaton. Susan came from the shadows. His friends are more than fond of Robin.

Still waters run deep, that's what the Master said about her. Because why? Because she was never bold. Because she didn't mix with the other girls. He had pointed his finger at her and waggled it a little. Still waters run deep, he said. There's more to Josephine Strane than meets the eye. He was right. And he hadn't wanted to let her go to Dr Casey's although he agreed in the end.

A moored boat emerges from the fog followed by part of the breakwater, then the cotton-grey closes again and there is no horizon, nothing against which to assess distance. Everything is remote and claustrophobic at the same time.

There is oil on the water, and pieces of timber and plastic milk bottles float in it. In sunshine there would be a rainbow in the oil if you looked at it from close down, from a certain angle, all the colours on the water. The oil makes everything slippery once your hands are wet. And it gets into your lungs, Auntie Mary said. Plenty of sailors drowned because they got oil in their lungs or the oil burned them inside.

Robin's hands are holding on to the edge of the boat when she pushes it a second time and he goes out with it, skewing the boat sideways towards himself, trailing in the water like a side-trawler's net. His red sweatshirt is almost black, a glistening fish-skin. His little face looks up at her and she takes pity on him.

Robin, she says, but she does not say it aloud, it has to be.

'Jo? Please?' Fear is the sound of his voice. His lips are shaking, his eyes are not blue any more, a darker colour that she could not name, as though she had looked into a room that was first illuminated and now was in darkness. Although she knows the same colours are there, there is darkness too. Now his whole body seems to be shaking. The boat tips down on his side and it seems to Josephine that the timbers of the boat are trembling in sympathy, tiny tremors that generate ripples where the strakes lap the water, the ripples spreading outwards, decaying as they go.

'Robin,' she says to him then. 'I love you.' The rush of love is almost too much for her. She gasps. She knows it is true. Robin is her child now. There is no going back. I'll be yours until we're old. This is what she was made for, this moment of joy. She thinks of the boyfriend who got her clothes open on the seat. She even looks towards it but only the concrete outline of the gents' is visible. He could not give her this. She thought of the scuffling and struggle and the indecent rubbing and pushing, the things he said, the noise. Robin was pure, delicate, an innocent, a doll, a bird. He would never do such things.

She makes a vow that she will never go for a boy again.

When Robin's hands slip and he drops down into the oil she is grateful. This is the painful part, she knows. Saying goodbye. The parting is harder when someone is lost at sea. There would be no body, only a name on a stone. Once a letter she read from Widow, Barnsley said: 'I grieve every day because he never came back to me.' Her husband was lost too. But what was the answer? Try to build a new life. Gone but not forgotten. But it is also true that the lost lover is safe for ever, free of danger. Now the catastrophe cannot reach him, down there beyond misfortune: in the liquid stillness he will be forever poised to return, never returning, expected but never found. His absence will fill the dead place, her longing for him will be a salve for the wound in her soul. Love, lost love will bring meaning to her existence. And his death will conserve the beauty of his life. He will never become coarse, never grow up to approach young girls in graveyards, to groan in the night in a nearby room, to push and rub and scuffle in the dark. Never grow old to lie rattling and mumbling in a hospital bed. Like the cold permafrost he will be constant and uncorrupted. Like the beautiful figures in his father's books. Snow White sleeping in perfection, never disturbed by the approaching prince.

Like Susan.

But Susan let water in at the eyes so never immerse the head. Death comes in there. Out of the shadow comes a bright face. You won't find your father here. Look what the nice man brought you.

Robin.

Watch out. Here comes the bogeyman.

The water is still again, the oil coagulating, forming delicate patterns, swirls and curls and planes of cobalt and petrel blue and aquamarine. The boat has calmed, riding on its painter on the glossy surface. She flicks the lighter one more time and notices that the flame is guttering. She stretches her hand out and lets the lighter go. It falls through the surface almost silently and for a brief moment it is gleaming and spinning against the cool green underworld. Then she looks round at the universe of fog and whispers goodbye. She feels better then.